THE STRETFORD ENDERS

SQUARE ONE

RED FOX

Also by Trevor J. Colgan:

The Stretford Enders
The Stretford Enders Away

THE STRETFORD ENDERS

SQUARE ONE

TREVOR J. COLGAN

RED FOX

THE STRETFORD ENDERS – SQUARE ONE
A RED FOX BOOK 009 943219 6

First published in Great Britain by Red Fox,
an imprint of Random House Children's Books

This edition published 2003

1 3 5 7 9 10 8 6 4 2

Papers used by Random House Children's Books are natural, recyclable products
made from wood grown in sustainable forests. The manufacturing processes
conform to the environmental regulations of the country of origin.

Set in Garamond by Falcon Oast Graphic Art Ltd.

Red Fox Books are published by Random House Children's Books,
61–63 Uxbridge Road, London W5 5SA,
a division of The Random House Group Ltd,
in Australia by Random House Australia (Pty) Ltd,
20 Alfred Street, Milsons Point, Sydney, NSW 2061, Australia,
in New Zealand by Random House New Zealand Ltd,
18 Poland Road, Glenfield, Auckland 10, New Zealand,
and in South Africa by Random House (Pty) Ltd,
Endulini, 5A Jubilee Road, Parktown 2193, South Africa.

THE RANDOM HOUSE GROUP Limited Reg. No. 954009
www.kidsatrandomhouse.co.uk

A CIP catalogue record for this book is available from the British Library.

Printed and bound in Great Britain by
Bookmarque Ltd, Croydon, Surrey

Contents

Dedicated to
Donncha MacCraith(1977–2002)
'A bright light taken from the world
far too early.'

Five Visitors Come to Town

Luke Farrell stepped onto the northbound platform of the Dun Laoghaire Dart station at ten past nine on Saturday morning. It had been drizzling steadily for over an hour. While he zipped up his tracksuit top, the Dart he had just left slowly pulled out of the station and snaked its way along the coast towards Monkstown. Luke adjusted the strap of his sports bag across his shoulder before climbing the steel staircase to the station exit. He handed his one-way ticket to the ticket collector and peered at the waiting 46A bus. The engine hummed rhythmically as a steady stream of passengers formed an orderly queue, waiting to board it. Luke sighed. Every time he reached Dun Laoghaire train station he would say a little prayer to himself. It was silly, really. But he preferred it if his bus, be it the 46A or the 75, was delayed. It gave him the perfect opportunity to stare across at 8 Montague Avenue and reminisce about happier times. He joined the growing queue to board the 46A and tipped the peak of his grey Nike baseball cap forward to deflect the tiny droplets of rain from his face. By the time he reached Woodlawn Comprehensive the drizzly downpour would have made the grass perfect for slick passing football. The kind of football that was currently tearing asunder the defences of every team in the South Dublin League, Division B.

Luke walked the half-mile from the bus stop to the gates of Woodlawn Comprehensive in a cage of concentration. His mother Martina, who was desperate for any opportunity to practise and improve her newly acquired driving skills, offered him a lift from Killiney each Saturday morning, but Luke had fallen into a successful routine. His pre-match stroll helped to clear his mind of everything apart from football. It was the same principle involved in stretching your muscles to warm up before a game. The walk had become a pivotal part of his preparation – a window of meditation before stepping onto the battlefield. It was proving extremely effective. The season was ten weeks old, but so far, the stats read: fifteen games, fifteen wins, thirty-three goals for Luke.

The Stretford Enders, spearheaded up front by Luke and from centre-midfield by a maturing Ille Popsecu, were destroying all before them. Their brand of fantasy football was attracting amorous attention from the weekly junior soccer supplements in the *Daily Star* and the *Evening Herald*, but more importantly, from eyes and ears across the Irish Sea. The sound of studs treading concrete knocked Luke out of his peaceful retreat. He stalled outside the iron gates and focused on the gang of unfamiliar faces lined up against a white Ford Transit van in the car park wearing canary-yellow shorts, socks and jerseys. They had to be Underwood Athletic, today's opposition. Luke diverted his attention to the pitch. A small crowd had gathered along the home side-line. Fathers, mothers, siblings and assorted friends. Four faces stuck out in this crowd like Toffees in the Kop.

'Villa, Spurs, Newcastle United and Man City,' a familiar deep voice said. Jerome was standing behind Luke. The vapour from his breath drifted up into the morning sky like smoke from a roaring chimney.

'The two old blokes by the corner flag?' Luke said.

'Arthur Moore and Reg Staines,' Jerome replied. 'Chief youth scouts with Villa and City.'

Luke nodded his head. He scanned further down the touchline. 'That blond bloke in the navy promo?' he said.

'Chris Rammell. Newcastle United,' Jerome replied.

Luke moved his head one more time. 'The small, baldy bloke next to Daniel?' he said.

'Terry Wise. Director of Tottenham's youth academy.'

Luke turned to face Jerome, who had his arms folded across his chest and wore a beaming smile of pride. 'I've even better news,' Jerome said.

Luke tried not to grin. Even better news than four top Premiership scouts turning up to watch him play had to be worth hearing. Jerome unwrapped two sticks of Juicy Fruit chewing gum before he proceeded with the explanation. Luke waited patiently to be offered some gum.

'Now, this is between me and you. Keep it under your hat, as they say,' Jerome said, handing Luke a stick of gum. He allowed him time to get a good chew going before starting to speak. Manager and player stared at one another, unable to conceal the smiles of delight.

'OK,' Jerome started, taking an early opportunity to catch a calming breath of oxygen. 'Terry called me last Thursday—'

'Terry Culshaw,' Luke said, interrupting.

Jerome nodded his head. 'Ever since you came back from Bellefield, he's been spreading the good word far and wide, keeping his ear to the ground . . .'

Terry Culshaw was the Everton scout who had spotted the talents of Luke, Tonka Matthews and David Swayne at the All-Ireland Cup Final three months earlier. He had brought them over to Merseyside for trials during the summer and encouraged both Luke and David to persevere with their dream despite the pain of rejection from Everton.

Of course, it was easy for a scout to issue such bland, inconsequential words of encouragement. But Terry Culshaw had done much more.

Jerome paused to swing his head left and right, just to check for pricked ears. He gripped Luke's left shoulder and moved a little closer.

'Now, Terry tells me Michael Turner has been keeping tabs on every game you've played this season. He sends a different scout each time to keep a low profile. But today, he's coming to check you out himself . . . and . . .' Jerome paused for air. He seemed too excited to say the words and his face subsided into a grin.

Luke urged him onwards with repeated nods of his head. 'Yeah?' he said anxiously.

Jerome finally let it out. 'He has a two-year pro contract for you to sign . . . today.'

Luke's knees buckled. He almost collapsed on the spot.

Jerome arched his head forward and spoke quietly into his left ear. 'Terry tells me the vibe surrounding you at the moment is red hot. He reckons at least two, and maybe all four, of the scouts here today will offer you a trial. That's why Turner has a contract: Preston want to beat the big boys to the punch.'

Suddenly, Luke felt a strange anxiety. He was confused. One offer was all he wanted. Five sounded like a headache of epic proportions. He looked to Jerome for advice. 'What do I do?' he said.

Jerome considered the question carefully. The serene sound of a steady downpour was all that broke the silence. Luke monitored his manager's thoughtful facial expression carefully. Finally, an answer.

'Terry reckons Preston's your best bet, and I agree with him,' he said.

Luke nodded. The opinions of Jerome Barnes and Terry Culshaw were more than enough for him. His mind was made up: he would put pen to paper and sign for Preston North End.

'It's a super set-up. Good manager, great supporters, nice stadium, First Division club, ambitious, you'll be on decent money, *and* you've got a much better chance to step up into the first team.'

Jerome's piled heap of reasons to sign for Preston North End were unnecessary. Luke had made up his mind without them. He trusted the word of Jerome and Terry more than anything else in the footballing world. He was certain they had his best interests at heart.

Luke smiled and stuck his hand out. 'Preston it is then,' he said.

Jerome glanced at the outstretched hand. At that moment he wanted to tell Luke how proud he made him feel. The positive manner in which he had reacted to the disappointment of Everton's rejection. After all, it wasn't easy for the lad. He had come within a whisker of a contract with a Premiership side – the very side he had supported all his life. The added agony of watching his best friend Tonka sign instead would have proven too much for some people. But not for Luke. He took a standing eight count and came out punching. The way in which he led his team by example, inspiring his fellow players to succeed by his own flawless performances.

Jerome wanted to say the words, 'I'm proud of you.' But the emotion was so overwhelming, he ran the risk of ending up a pathetic ball of tears and slobber. He decided instead on a safer bet: actions speaker louder than words. Luke let out an animated 'Oaf' as Jerome snatched him up into the air in a monstrous bear hug. He was elevated high above the ground for fifteen seconds before being dumped back to earth.

Jerome puffed out a jaded groan. 'You're too heavy for that kind of horseplay,' he said defensively.

Luke wore a smug smile. He patted his manager on the back as they walked on towards the dressing rooms. 'You're getting old, boss. You're getting old,' he said.

It was quarter past ten when Jerome handed Luke the match ball and held open the dressing-room door for him to lead his side out onto the field of play.

'From the start, Enders, from the start,' Robert Nally shouted enthusiastically. Nally was one of five summer signings brought in to help strengthen a squad robbed of two of its most influential players during the close season. Tall, athletic, skilful and eager to impress, Nally was the perfect replacement for Tonka Matthews. Luke and the Enders trotted out onto the pitch to a healthy round of applause from the crowd, which had doubled in size over the course of the last hour. Underwood Athletic were already waiting to start the match.

'Luke,' Jerome shouted from the touchline.

Luke turned away from Ille, who was waiting in the centre-circle with him to tip off. Jerome was standing beside a tall, dark-haired man in his thirties. He gestured for Luke to join them. Luke located the referee, who was busy checking the opposition's boots and shin guards on the edge of their own penalty area. He spun back to Ille.

'Hold tight, Ille,' Luke said. He jogged across to join Jerome and the mystery man.

'Luke, this is Michael Turner, Preston North End's youth team coach,' Jerome said. Michael Turner offered his hand and a friendly smile. Luke reciprocated.

'Pleased to meet you, Mr Turner,' he said politely.

'It's a pleasure, Luke,' Turner replied. Up close and personal, Michael Turner was a far friendlier prospect. His smile revealed two rows of straight and spotless teeth and a pair of piercing blue eyes. He wore a plain navy Umbro tracksuit over a lean, wiry physique. This was a man in the peak of physical fitness.

'Sorry for pulling you out of the game, Luke, but I was wondering if Jerome, you and your mother would like to join me for dinner tonight to discuss terms,' Turner said.

Luke openly glanced at Jerome for advice.

Jerome nodded his head.

'Yeah, sure,' Luke replied.

Turner smiled. 'Great, we'll sort out the details after the match.'

Luke hesitated for a second or so before jogging back to the centre-circle. Only now was it starting to sink in. He'd done it, he'd won himself a contract with a professional football team. The referee perched the whistle in his mouth when Luke arrived back at the centre-circle. Ille put his left boot on the ball and nodded to Luke as he prepared to roll it across to him. Luke couldn't help but smile. It was time for a joyous celebration.

Underwood Athletic meant business. The fearsome reputation of a marauding Stretford Enders side preceded them. Every game they had played in that season they dominated and destroyed the opposition. Athletic were determined to stand toe-to-toe and fight. Hence, the first fifteen minutes saw a rash of clumsy, mistimed tackles and acts of crude physical intimidation. Although the score remained nil–nil, the punishing pace of constantly pressurising the ball was sapping the energy of the Athletic back four.

'Mark up,' the number four screamed to his team-mates. He was built like a polar bear with a penchant for seal meat and snarled with the same menace. This huge creature had obviously been detailed to man-mark Luke. He followed him all over the pitch, snapping at his heels, tugging his jersey, growling in his ear.

'Ille,' Luke yelled.

The little Romanian wizard laid a ball into Luke's path, ten yards outside the penalty area. The number four swung a huge tree trunk of a leg at Luke, but his lumbering swipe caught nothing but fresh air. With a dizzying change of pace, Luke spun his marker before weaving his way past three hopeless challenges, into the penalty area. The goalkeeper rushed forward to narrow the angle, but was nutmegged for his trouble. Luke jogged back to the centre-circle, receiving the congratulations of his team-mates and a warm round of applause from the crowd. Ille ambushed him from behind, taking a running jump onto his back.

'You so greedy, you pass once a while,' Ille insisted.

Luke laughed. Ille's sense of humour was coming on a lot faster than his English. They continued towards the halfway line in jockey-back mode.

After the restart, Underwood Athletic lost their shape, their concentration and their self-belief. This did seem inevitable once the first goal went in, but it was still staggering how easily Luke and his team-mates tore them to shreds. For the remainder of the first half the Enders passed the ball from left to right, back to front, then back again – merely toying with their defenceless opponents. Luke, Copper and Ille were the ball players in the side. Aided by the tireless running of Nally they orchestrated the pace and the pattern of play. This arrogant tactic went hand in hand with the knowledge that they had the ability to score goals at will. In the final minute of the first half Copper Martin carried the ball from the edge of his own penalty area, unchallenged, to the halfway line before swinging a crossfield pass from left to right. Nally controlled it beautifully, trapping the ball with his first touch. Luke screamed one word.

'Now.'

Nally was alive to the call and zipped the ball with the outside of his right boot into the channel between the left-back and the number four. Luke turned and darted clear, the bulky number four struggling to make up the ground. As he entered the right side of the penalty area diagonally, the number five and number six moved across his path, attempting to block off his route to goal. This defensive move actually gave him the angle he was looking for. With the minimum of fuss, Luke wrapped his left boot around the ball and curled it sweetly into the top left-hand corner. The keeper froze on the spot, watching in disbelief.

Copper Martin and Muffin Burke sprinted sixty yards to join in the celebrations. Luke smiled as they held his left leg aloft and pretended to polish his boot. The ref blew his whistle seconds after Underwood Athletic kicked off. Two–nil at half time. The game was dead as a dodo.

'Great ball, Rob,' Luke said to Nally as he trotted off the pitch. Nally patted his captain on the back. 'Come on, boys, keep it going,' Luke continued.

He stood on the sideline, congratulating all his players, Les, Lofty, the Burke brothers, Edgar, Alan Giles. Emotion was welling in his eyes and throat. This could be his last game for the Stretford Enders, the team of no-hopers he had helped to mould into champions.

'It's looking like sixteen for sixteen, Skip,' Copper Martin said happily. He and Ille were the last players to leave the field of play. Luke smiled and joined them in walking towards the dressing rooms. Along the way, he noticed Jerome and Michael Turner standing outside the main door, deep in conversation. Luke turned his head one hundred eighty degrees. On the far side of the field, the four youth team scouts were kicking a ball about, sharing a laugh and a joke. This was a reality. He was on his way to professional football.

Jerome's half-time team talks had gradually, over a period of time, become much calmer affairs. Especially now his team swept aside all before them. Phrases such as 'keep tracking back', 'concentration', 'pass and move' had become staple fare. Simple words of encouragement to maintain performance, not radically improve it. Luke sat in a corner of the dressing room, sipping from a bottle of Lucozade Sport. He turned his head slowly to soak up every detail of the room, the faces munching bananas, the red-tiled floor, the kit bag sitting on the massage table, the wooden benches, the metal coat hangers running round the wall. He felt a warm sense of nostalgia.

'Come on, Enders. Let's get this job done right,' Nally screamed, breaking Luke's concentration.

The Enders roared in unison. Luke snapped out of his daydream and stood up to lead his team back onto the pitch. Underwood Athletic slumped back out of their dressing room in dejected fashion.

'If this were a boxing match, the ref would've stopped it by now,' Copper said to Luke as they jogged onto the pitch.

'Don't get too comfy, Copper. A lot can happen in forty-five minutes,' Nally said, overhearing the comment.

Luke was greatly impressed by this reprimand. He looked at Nally, clapping his hands together to rally the troops. He felt a sudden sense of security: the baton of responsibility was being passed on to a worthy generation. The second half of the match kicked off with Underwood Athletic staging a rare attack. The rain had stopped just long enough for the crowd on the sideline to put down their umbrellas and unbuckle the hoods of their rain jackets. Luke tried not to glance at the chorus line of scouts, realising concentration was an important quality for potential professional footballers to display. He did keep an occasional tab on Michael Turner, but the names and faces of the other scouts seemed to pass into obscurity as the Enders regained their stranglehold on the match.

Luke drifted into space on the left wing. He raised his right hand high in the air. 'Ille,' he called.

Ille turned the number six inside out before chipping a delightful ball from the centre-circle to Luke on the left wing. Even as he controlled the ball on his chest, he could sense the palpable struggle of the opposition defence in turning to chase after him. Against such feeble resistance, he forged forward to the edge of the penalty area before smacking a fierce drive low to the keeper's right. Three–nil to the Enders. It was all too easy. As if by magic, the sun barged its way past a thick buffer of mucky rain clouds to brighten up the morning. Luke and Ille responded to this meteorological provocation and exposed some sloppy defending. Underwood Athletic had lost all spirit, allowing Ille two clear-cut chances in front of goal, which he duly dispatched with natural aplomb.

Five–nil up with four minutes to play. The Enders saved the best goal till last. As the second half progressed, Nally had started pushing into midfield more to link up the play. After exchanging a neat one-two with Copper Martin on the halfway line, Nally released Lofty O'Keefe down the right wing with a measured pass. The powerful winger had developed a useful touch since joining the Enders two years back. He easily outpaced the left-back to knock a wonderful first-time cross to the near post. Luke shrugged off the by now lethargic advances of the number four to glance an acute header towards the far post. The ball nestled in the bottom corner of the net.

Six–nil.

Luke made a special detour to thank Lofty O'Keefe for his sublime centre. Afterwards he jogged back down the sideline, where Michael Turner stood applauding with a satisfied smile.

Underwood Athletic prepared to kick off. Shoulders slumped, faces frowning, hands firmly on hips – it would be fair to say they were none too enthusiastic about playing on into injury time. The referee blew his whistle and the number nine knocked the ball sideways to the number ten, who immediately miscontrolled this basic pass.

Luke sprinted from his position outside the centre-circle to challenge for the ball. He put his right foot forward to block tackle, forcing the number ten to try and muscle past him. With the ball forming the meat of the sandwich, it was a simple case of he who dares, wins. Luke stood up strong, blocking the number ten from moving past with the ball and forcing him to reassert his balance. But instead of swerving out of the way, the number ten collided straight into Luke, knocking him down. The two players were wrapped in a heap on the ground.

'Sorry, mate,' the number ten said sincerely.

Luke stared at the sky, biting his tongue as the searing pain shot from his right leg through his abdomen and chest like a scorching hot fireball. Only he had heard the awful sound of the snap.

A Clean Break

Somehow, none of it seemed real. The conversation with Jerome, the match against Underwood Athletic, the scouts, Michael Turner, the six goals, the block tackle. Luke quickly convinced himself it was all part of a bad dream, a nightmare. As far as he was concerned, Friday night ended when he turned off the TV in his bedroom after watching *Raw Is War* on Sky Sports One. He was now, and had been, asleep. Allowing his cynical mind to dream up a worst-case scenario to punish him for his behaviour that summer, he saw that there was a fitting sense of irony in this form of retribution. Egotistical prima donna denied the chance to parade the immense sporting talent he believed made him superior to mere mortals. It was a striking message from the cosmos. You're nothing special. Unfortunately, reality runs on a tight schedule. There was a knock on the door of his hospital room.

'Can I come in?' Jerome said from outside.

Luke gulped in despair. 'Yeah,' he replied weakly.

Jerome stepped inside and closed the door gently behind him. Luke made no effort to sit up straight in bed. He preferred to stare at the ceiling and keep his right leg in the elevated position Dr Singh had suggested to help the blood flow freely. Jerome sat down on the edge of the bed and stared Luke in the eye.

'It's not the end of the world,' he said. He was well aware

such a glib comment would do little to lift Luke's spirits. But he had countless plausible, logical points to back up his statement.

'Look, ninety per cent of professional players get a bad injury sometime in their career.'

'I'm not a professional,' Luke replied sadly.

This fact was undeniable. It stopped Jerome dead in his tracks. Michael Turner had brought a professional contract ready to be signed, but no football club in the world would sign a player without them passing a medical first. The shared anxiety flowing from player to manager at that precise moment revolved around the x-rays Dr Singh had taken a half-hour earlier.

Jerome stared at Luke, a horrible sensation of déjà vu curling down his spine. He remembered sitting in a similar, sterile hospital room in Manchester, seventeen years earlier. Staring at identical whitewashed walls, mulling over the same misfortune. Coming to terms with his dream slipping through his fingers like sand. Luke was a creature fashioned from the same mould as Jerome Barnes. Football meant everything to them; it always had and always would. Playing, watching, talking about. It was the driving force behind their childhoods, the one thing that could always be counted upon to make life bearable.

And now, in a cruel twist of fate, the dream was about to be snatched away from Luke in the same way it had been ripped away from Jerome.

'You must be frozen,' Jerome said. He jumped off the bed and shut the window behind Luke, which was letting in a frosty October breeze fit to chill. He caught a fleeting glance at the landscape behind St James's Hospital. An unruly row of dour granite buildings dotted with grime-encrusted windows, a blanket of dishwater rain clouds overhead showering the litter-strewn streets with a malignant acidic drizzle.

Luke quickly became aware of Jerome's desire to avoid his eyes. He needed to ask the question, no matter how badly he never wanted to hear the answer. 'How did you get over it?' he said quietly.

Jerome, who had skulked into a corner to tune in the TV, finally turned to face him. 'You don't need to know that. You'll recover from this, kid. I guarantee it,' he insisted.

Luke wanted desperately to believe him. But Jerome could not make that guarantee. They both knew it. Football throughout the ages was littered with players who lost out on great careers through injury. Players who recovered but were never the same physical force upon their return. Prone to niggles, unable to build up the stamina levels they were capable of beforehand. The invisible entity that serious injury cost an athlete was momentum, and anyone who ever took part in sport seriously would understood what a vital weapon in the arsenal this was for all top-class competitors.

Luke decided to ask the question again. 'Please, boss. Just tell me what's it like,' he said softly.

Jerome stared at him with a sombre expression. He loved Luke like a son. He couldn't bear lying to him. It hurt having to say the words, but it was a simple choice. Tell the truth, or leave him to face reality unprepared. He gulped ominously before composing himself, sorting out the dreadful feeling that, even to this day, lingered in the dark recesses of his mind.

'It's a pain that never goes away. You *will* learn to live with it. But it never stops stinging.'

Luke could feel the tears rolling down his cheeks. Jerome watched this sad display, not in the least bit embarrassed. He understood completely, better than anyone else in the world.

Without hesitation, he moved across to the bed and held Luke in his arms. He offered the comfort and shoulder that neither Luke's mother Martina nor his girlfriend Ella would be able to provide. While they embraced, Dr Singh, a small middle-aged Indian man, entered the room wearing a long white doctor's coat over a blue surgeon's gown. He carried with him the results of the x-ray.

Luke and Jerome turned in unison, but neither had the guts to ask the question. Dr Singh pre-empted the inevitable with a give-away smile.

'I have some good news,' he said. He took a sheet of plastic from a brown folder and clipped it onto the x-ray light box. He flicked a nearby switch which provided fluorescent light to illuminate the x-ray. With a black Bic biro in hand, the doctor pointed to the graph.

'Clean break of the shinbone,' he said. 'Three months in plaster.' Dr Singh was done explaining. He turned off the light switch and placed the x-ray back inside the brown folder.

'Doc,' Jerome said anxiously, 'what about football?'

Dr Singh puffed out a weary sigh. 'Well, I *do* fancy Palace for promotion, myself,' he said with a wry smile.

Jerome and Luke handled the comment with semi-serious frowns. Dr Singh quickly clarified.

'Once the cast is off, I can't see any problems. In fact, this break should strengthen the bone.'

It was the kind of news Jerome didn't dare pray for when Luke keeled over on the pitch that morning. He smothered his star player with a loving hug and kiss to the temple before leaping to his feet to shake hands with Dr Singh and offer him his eternal thanks and a fifty-pound voucher for Barnes' Sports Store.

Once the doctor departed, the gloomy hospital room

turned into a scene of celebration to rival the Tolka Park dressing room after the All-Ireland Cup Final victory over Stella Maris. The disappointment of breaking a leg became negligible. Luke could recover; it wasn't the end end. And that was something worth celebrating.

An Endless Parade of Well-Wishers

After the visit of Dr Singh, Jerome was a pocket of nervous energy. He paced about the room, talking of his respect and reverence for medical practitioners before making a hasty exit to the hospital shop to pick up some supplies. He left the room promising to 'sort some things out', as he put it, along the way. Luke took the opportunity for respite as heaven sent. The fear and anxiety caused by the prospect of never playing football again had left him bereft of energy. His plan for the evening was simple. Dinner followed by sleep. Unfortunately, his accident would bring with it a procession of visitors curious to check on his health. He took several deep breaths to stiffen his resolve, consoling himself with the thought that Saturday night had to end at some point.

Jerome was the first person to burst through the door. 'Right,' he said abruptly. 'I've been in touch with the scouts. They asked me to call when I had an update on your condition.'

This news did raise Luke's interest a little. He attempted to sit up straight in bed. Jerome dumped a white plastic bag on a nearby chair before coming to his aid.

'What did they say?' Luke said anxiously.

Jerome busied himself fluffing pillows. 'Well, they all went out of their way to express serious interest in signing you. However, before they even think about offering you a trial, they want to see you back in action next spring.'

Luke shuffled about on the bed until he found a comfortable position. Jerome reached across and picked up the plastic bag. He emptied a two-litre bottle of 7-Up, a big bag of grapes, a BLT sandwich and a copy of *FourFourTwo* magazine onto the mattress.

'So, anyway, I arranged for them to visit on the tenth of April next year – that's my prediction for your comeback game. They all want to come see you play.'

Luke munched his way through the bunch of grapes. 'What about Michael Turner?' he said, between chews and swallows.

'We'll talk about that later,' Jerome replied. He got out of the chair and walked to the door. Before leaving he turned to look at Luke. 'I rang your mum and Ella. I said I'd pick them up. Oh, and the lads want to drop by later.'

Luke nodded his head in agreement. Jerome smiled.

'See you later, kid,' he said happily.

Jerome closed the door behind him. Luke picked up the TV remote control from the bedside cabinet and flicked onto Sky Sports One. It was quarter past three and the results service from *Sports Saturday* was already in full flow. Luke scanned the screen for Everton's score. They were drawing nil–nil with Aston Villa at Goodison Park. Luke yawned. He was still exhausted, but planned to battle his fatigue and keep an eye on the progress of his beloved Toffees.

Luke fell asleep sometime between quarter to and four o'clock. He fought bravely to keep an eye on the Everton score line, but his body finally gave up with the fading autumn daylight outside his window. It was a strong possibility he would have slept through till Monday morning if left undisturbed, but his brief slumber was broken by a knock on the door.

'Luke?' an unfamiliar voice called from outside.

It took Luke a while to find his bearings. He straightened up in bed before mumbling, 'Come in.'

The door opened slowly to reveal an unexpected visitor.

'Mr Turner,' Luke said in surprise. Michael Turner shut the door behind him and walked across to the chair by Luke's bed. He had a Champion Sports plastic bag in his hand.

'Can I have a seat?' he said politely. Luke nodded and reached across to flick on the bedside table lamp. Michael sat down and took a good look at the plaster cast on Luke's right leg.

'Is the pain bad?' he said.

Luke shook his head.

'I fractured my collarbone in the play-off final at Wembley in 'ninety-two. I had to play fifty minutes with a sling round my right arm,' Michael said.

Jerome had never mentioned the fact Michael was a former professional. Luke listened intently to his would-be manager's wonderful story of bravery.

'We were two–one down with a minute to go when Billy French equalised. Soon as he scored I started cursing his name. All I wanted to do was get to hospital—'

'Did you play on?' Luke said, interrupting.

Michael nodded. 'No choice in the matter, we'd already used up all our substitutes. By the end of extra time I was seeing double. When the final whistle blew I fainted. The next thing I remember was waking up in hospital.'

Luke smiled and remembered what Jerome said to him earlier. Ninety per cent of all professionals suffer some sort of serious injury. It actually made him feel a sense of pride: he was now a fully paid-up member of the injury club.

'Oh, I popped into town and got this for you. I thought

you might need cheering up,' Michael said. He handed Luke the Champion Sports bag. It was only polite to ask before opening up, but Michael was already urging him on.

'Go on, it's an injury gift,' he said.

Luke dipped his hands inside and pulled out a green jersey. It was the new Ireland top. Fifty quid's worth. Luke was a little overwhelmed. 'Thanks, Mr Turner,' he said sincerely.

'That's not all,' Michael replied. Luke looked at him in confusion. After a few seconds he dipped his hands back inside the bag and searched about. He gripped some stapled pages and slowly pulled them out. He studied the first page carefully. It was emblazoned with the crest of Preston North End. His two-year professional contract.

Luke looked up at Michael Turner in astonishment.

'Two hundred pounds a week. Free accommodation. First-team bonus, win bonus, goal bonus and a pay review after each six-month period,' Michael said.

Luke was silent. What a depressing moment. He was listening to the details of his bright future in football, which had been snatched away by a foolish block tackle in the dying minutes of a nothing game.

'Luke, I'm not showing you this to rub your nose in it. As far as I'm concerned, that deal still applies. However, I'm sure your manager has let you know about the need to pass a medical,' Michael said.

Luke turned his eyes to his chest and nodded his head.

'However . . .' Michael said.

Luke looked up instantly. Michael Turner was holding a silver ballpoint pen.

'As an act of faith, I want you to sign that contract. That means, as soon as your leg is out of plaster, I'll come see you play with the club doctor, conduct an on-the-spot medical.

When you pass, you'll be a Preston North End player.'

Michael offered Luke the pen. 'It's as simple as this, Luke. You are the most promising young talent I've seen in twenty years. I'm determined to bring you to Preston North End.'

Luke had nothing to think about. Jerome approved, Terry Culshaw approved. The Ireland jersey, the kind visit and the words of encouragement simply copper-fastened the deal. He took the pen and signed for Preston North End.

Michael stayed on another twenty minutes. Before he left St James's Hospital he told Luke about his plans for the youth team at Preston. It was an exciting conversation which left him awash with optimism and a calming sense of security.

'Take care, Luke. I'll call you in a week or so,' Michael said as he stood up to leave.

Luke sat up to shake his hand. 'Thanks, Mr Turner. I won't let you down,' he said.

Michael Turner smiled. 'Do me a favour. Don't take up snooker while you're in that plaster.'

Luke laughed. He watched Michael Turner leave the room. It seemed like a matter of mere seconds before Martina and Ella burst in and rugby-tackled him with debilitating hugs. He struggled for air as an overload of TLC threatened to cause an injury worse than the one inflicted by the block tackle that morning.

'My baby, my poor baby,' Martina said, sobbing sadly.

Luke sighed at his mother, who couldn't help but cry. Ella stood beside her: she wasn't on the verge of tears but there was a definite suggestion of anxiety in her downtrodden frown. Luke groaned.

'Stop it, Ma. I'm fine,' he said defiantly.

Martina tried to curtail her sobbing, but tears continued to stream down her cheeks each time she glanced at the thick white plaster cast wrapped round his injured right leg. Jerome and his wife Mo were next to arrive with the entire Enders squad in tow. Luke sat up straight and prepared himself for the barrage of questions. It was going to be a long evening.

The Enders didn't outstay their welcome. A quick chat, a couple of magazines and a massive bag of grapes bought for comic effect and they were gone. Martina, Jerome and Mo headed home at half seven, leaving Luke and Ella. Alone at last. They had a date that evening. Ella had bought tickets for them to go see Morcheeba at the Olympia. Instead, they snuggled up together on the bed watching *The Simpsons* on Sky One. Ella glanced at his leg.

'Does it hurt?' she said.

Luke was more concerned with asking a question of his own before answering hers. 'Is anyone else going to that gig tonight?'

Ella turned towards him. 'Like who?' she said coyly.

'Isaac, the Starfish . . . Weasel – I mean Wesley,' Luke said smugly.

Ella sat up straight. He could sense the guilty desire in her eyes. In fairness, she had been looking forward to the Morcheeba gig for months. It wasn't exactly her fault he broke his leg. Her big brother Isaac and the Funky Starfish – Ella's backing band – were massive fans of Morcheeba and never missed a gig they played in Dublin. Hence their absence from the list of hospital visitors.

'What time were we supposed to meet them?' Luke said.

Ella lay down on his chest. 'It doesn't matter,' she replied.

'What time?' Luke reaffirmed.

Ella sat up again. She stared into Luke's eyes with a sombre expression. She had something to say, but it wasn't to

23

do with the Morcheeba gig. 'I have something to tell you,' she faltered.

Suddenly Luke was in a state of panic. This sounded bad – by tone of voice alone. He gulped loudly as Ella prepared to impart her news. He watched her mouth carefully for the shape of 'Wes'. If her explanation started with the w-word, Luke was in a whole heap of trouble.

'Wesley was in London last week,' Ella said. This was a mere teaser. Luke urged her on.

'Yeah, and . . .'

'Well, he had a meeting with a record company. Fab Note Records,' Ella explained. She stopped again. But this time her anxious frown turned to a happy grin.

'They want to sign me and the Funky Starfish. They've offered us a three-album deal,' she said excitedly.

Luke switched to automatic. He laughed happily, threw his arms round her and squeezed her tight. He had been preparing himself for this eventuality ever since they reconciled in August. His pre-recorded speech went along the lines of 'Ella, that's brilliant. I'm so proud of you.' Luke had thought this one through carefully. If he signed for a football team, Ella would be expected to act in a certain way. If she signed a record deal, he would do the same. There could be no half measures, no hedging of bets or sitting on the fence. It was all or nothing in this situation. If he didn't play the thrilled boyfriend part to perfection, she would smell his spite a mile off.

'So, when do you start recording?' Luke said. He was a sudden hive of energy, asking questions, smiling profusely. Thankfully, Ella bought his ploy hook, line and sinker.

'Well, we fly to London tomorrow to sign the deal,' she explained enthusiastically. 'Then we'll have a strategy meeting, sort out studio time for demos, a marketing plan, showcase gigs, photo shoots, publicity stunts . . .'

Luke's initial reaction was bad. He harboured fear and mistrust in the pit of his stomach. It seemed like the gods were conspiring against him again. Fate and incident had dealt him a rotten hand. Ella lands a record deal the same day he breaks his leg. Somehow, he doubted the chance of coincidence. Midway through her rundown of the London trip itinerary, she got a call on her mobile. It was Weasel. Luke sat back and listened. It was an enquiry about the Morcheeba gig. He would have to let her leave. He knew the game had changed. They were playing by a whole different set of rules. Ever since that July evening in Montague Avenue when he allowed her to fall to the floor, 'he and Ella' had altered for ever. When she said goodbye to Weasel, even before she opened her mouth to ask him, Luke conceded defeat.

'Go on,' he said with a smile.

Ella didn't second-guess him. She leaned forward and kissed him on the lips with an audible smack.

'I love you, Farrell,' she said, staring deeply into his eyes. Luke didn't reply. He chose instead to watch her rush from his room to meet up with her band and manager for a well-earned celebration. Before she was long gone he looked to the door and posed the question.

'Do you?' he said quietly. All that was left was silence. Luke had no desire to watch *Match of the Day*. He would tune into *Goals on Sunday* on Sky Sports One the next evening. For now, he snuggled up with his two-year pro contract and slept.

Sunday was a day of rest. Luke sat in bed watching telly. He escaped with a mere hour of motherly attention from Martina. Ella and the Starfish had been to see Morcheeba at the Olympia by way of celebration. Today, after dealing with their respective hangovers, they had to pack for the big trip to London. Therefore Luke accepted Ella's absence as unavoidable when Jerome called in alone that evening. Although he told himself it was OK, that he didn't mind her staying away, it was a lie. Luke could sense a change in her, it was undeniable. But as he spent Sunday night awake, alone, soul-searching, he came to the conclusion that things with Ella hadn't been right for some time.

Dr Singh called in to Luke's room on Monday morning to sign his release papers.

'Now, you must take it easy for the first couple of weeks. Try and walk as little as possible,' he insisted.

Luke paraded a cheeky smile. 'That sounds good to me, Doc,' he replied.

The idea of being waited on hand and foot did have an appealing ring to it. When Dr Singh signed the papers and finally stopped harping on about the resurgence of the mighty Eagles in Division One, he wished Luke good luck with his recovery.

Luke sat alone on his bed, carefully examining his new crutches. After that he peered down at his cast, observing with pride the vast list of names and messages scribbled on the plaster in various colours. It was vain to assess your importance by the amount of graffiti smeared across a plaster cast, but he concluded he was a popular character.

'Hi,' Martina said.

Luke turned his attention to the door. Martina stood there, smiling. Beside her was a pretty teenage girl wearing flared blue jeans, navy Adidas Samba trainers and a pink T-shirt with the words 'PORN STAR' emblazoned across the chest. She also had piercings in her nose, in her right eyebrow, through her tongue and God knows where else. She was smallish, very shapely and had toasted blonde hair tied in a bun.

'Ready to go?' Martina said.

Luke didn't reply verbally. He simply nodded his head shyly.

Martina quickly remembered her manners. 'Oh, sorry. Luke, this is Jude, my new assistant,' she said.

'Hi,' Jude said, raising her hand in greeting.

Between them, Martina and Jude picked up the line of plastic bags on the bed and waited for Luke to employ his crutches. Martina watched anxiously as her little boy got to grips with his new toys.

'Can you manage, sweetheart? I can ask the doctor for a wheelchair,' she said.

Luke stared her through. 'Ma, don't start, OK?' he said bluntly.

Martina wasn't aware of her embarrassing behaviour. Luke struggled out the front door with his mother and Jude trailing behind. In an ideal world, his simple warning would have been heeded, but in reality he knew he was set for a *long* journey home. Jude and the poor, unsuspecting taxi man were treated to an episode of 'My Son the Superstar'. The groans of derision from Luke did little to dissuade his mother. She continued to drone on about his professional contract with Preston North End and the swarm of Premiership teams chasing his signature. The only slight relief arrived in the form of Jude's wry smile. She displayed real empathy – understanding only too well the agony of an overbearing parent. When they reached Killiney, she helped Luke inside while Martina paid the taxi man and explained how to use the intercom to get out past the security gates.

'Sorry about all that crap,' Luke said as he showed Jude his bedroom.

'Ahh, I think it's sweet. She's so proud of you. You should hear her in the canteen at work,' Jude replied.

Luke almost tripped over his crutches. 'At work?' he said anxiously.

Jude smiled. She placed the collection of plastic bags in a neat pile at the bottom of Luke's bed. It was at this point the patio window caught her attention.

'Wow,' she said, gasping unashamedly. She walked to within inches of the glass to soak up the view.

'Not bad, is it?' Luke said.

'Not bad?' Jude replied. 'It's amazing. I'd love to take some shots up here,' she added.

Luke walked over to her side and stared down at Killiney Bay below. It *was* a wonderful view, provided by the property's elevated site, close to the top of Killiney Head. A few seconds passed by, just enough for quiet contemplation, but well short of awkward silence.

'You're a photographer?' Luke said.

Jude kept her eyes trained on the beach below. 'Yeah, well, I'm studying photography in Dun Laoghaire Art College. Boots helps to pay the bills.'

Jude finished her survey of the panoramic view. She turned to Luke and smiled her friendly smile. 'I'd better get back to work,' she said.

Luke sat down on his bed. 'It was nice to meet you, Jude. Thanks for your help,' he said.

Jude waved goodbye before walking down the hallway to report to Martina. Luke employed one of his crutches to poke his bedroom door shut before turning his attention to the TV. He could still make out the muffled conversation between Martina and Jude. Then he heard the front door open and shut.

Martina appeared in his bedroom seconds later. 'Everything OK?' she said.

Luke stared at her in surprise. 'Why aren't you heading back to work?' he asked abruptly.

'Work? I'm not setting foot outside this door. There's no way I'm leaving you alone in *your* condition.' It was an ominous statement. Martina walked across to Luke, stripped him of his crutches and tidied them away in a wardrobe. He watched her potter about his room, holding in a deeply anxious groan. She finally left the bedroom five minutes later, giving Luke the chance to channel-hop. Daytime TV was abominable. After a fleeting flick through the terrestrials and a brief pause on MTV to soak up the latest Atomic Kitten video, he settled on Nickelodeon. He planned to watch *Thomas the Tank Engine & Friends*, purely for nostalgia, until the sports bulletin on Sky News at twenty past twelve.

Fifteen minutes later, while Luke watched with bated breath to see the outcome of cheeky Percy's plan to go past a DANGER sign on the harbour wharf, a distinct aroma wafted through his bedroom door. A pungent stink of . . .

'Chicken soup,' Martina announced happily. She stood at

the door holding a tray. Luke lurched backwards in horror as she plonked a steaming bowl of chicken broth beneath his nostrils.

'What's this?' he said loudly.

Martina looked at him in confusion. 'Chicken soup,' she replied, handing him a spoon.

'I know it's chicken soup. What's it doing here?' Luke said impatiently. The point he was trying to make was, he had a broken shinbone, not the flu.

Martina's feelings were bruised. 'You don't want it?' she said sadly.

Luke suddenly felt guilty. He often complained about Martina working long hours and studying late at night. He would moan about the lack of attention he received. Now she was making a *real* effort. He could not ignore her clumsy attempts at TLC. They demanded some ego pampering. He grabbed the spoon and sank it to the bottom of the bowl. He supped the scalding hot broth with great vigour. It was a simple gesture and one that restored the smile to his mother's face immediately.

'Would you like some buttered bread for dunking?' she said eagerly.

Luke nodded his head enthusiastically. Although his tolerance of the chicken soup was a measure designed to appease in the short term, he knew his mother too well – given an inch she'd take a mile. This small sign of encouragement had given her carte blanche to smother him with love.

Luke glanced at the alarm clock on his bedside cabinet. 'Two more hours of sanity,' he said, by way of prediction.

* * *

It was actually four hours before Luke lost all reason. His bed was a mountain of pillows, fluffed to their fullest. Glasses or cups of 7-Up, water, soup and orange juice lined the bedside cabinet. The radiator had been turned on full blast since eight that morning. All this was unsettling enough without Martina's regular meander through his bedroom. Every ten minutes she would make her entrance, block the TV, sit on his bed, chat away about school, Ella, Boots and, worst of all, her boyfriend Jonathan D'Argo. Luke had taken all he could handle. He needed to free himself from her unwitting torture chamber.

'Listen, Ma, maybe you should go back to work,' he suggested.

'No,' Martina replied steadfastly.

Luke manoeuvred himself from beneath the confines of the tightly wrapped duvet, which had started to stem the circulation of blood in the lower half of his body. Martina watched in horror as he stood up straight, using the cabinet as a makeshift crutch.

'What are you doing?' she said.

'I'm going out,' Luke replied.

'Out?' Martina gasped.

Luke was determined to see it through. He tracked his way around the room, employing the wall as a handrail of sorts. Martina, for all her good intentions, didn't exactly jump to his aid.

'Out where?' she demanded.

Luke was closing in on the wardrobe. He had been thinking about this one carefully, and there was only one person to go visit. 'I'm calling over to see David,' he said.

Martina sighed anxiously. Luke was expecting a verbal argument. Instead, he was able to retrieve the first crutch without any attempt on his mother's part to abort his planned trip in the preliminary stages. To his complete surprise, she stood up and helped him reach the second crutch.

'I'll give you a lift,' she said.

'No, Ma, I'll get the Dart,' Luke replied immediately.

Martina faced him, not with wounded pride, but with mild curiosity. She seemed to be weighing up a question in her mind while Luke steadied himself on the crutches. He stared at her, awaiting the enquiry.

'Why David?' she asked. It was a fair question. Luke hadn't seen David Swayne outside of school in over a month. In August he had dropped a major bombshell by leaving the Stretford Enders and since then had become a virtual recluse.

'Because I need to talk to him,' Luke replied. He was anxious to escape the claustrophobic climes of his bedroom and his mother as quickly as possible. Answering a barrage of questions would only delay his exit.

Martina trailed Luke as he hopped down the hall towards the front door. 'Take a jacket, and call if you get into trouble,' she insisted.

Luke grabbed his Everton rain jacket from the antique mahogany coat hanger inside the front door. He backed up into the kitchen and took his Walkman and wallet from the long kitchen counter, stuffing them into the jacket pockets.

Martina opened the front door. 'Be careful,' she said.

Luke tried to ghost past without a peck on the cheek – unsuccessfully. As he hopped down the long, winding tarmac driveway towards the security gates, he could sense his mother standing by the open door, watching her baby anxiously. He arched his neck backwards and surveyed the greyscale sky overhead. Rain was imminent, some might say inevitable. But he had no intention of returning home until late that evening, whatever the weather. A torrential downpour sounded far more appealing than another bowl of scalding hot chicken soup.

David Swayne was one of the finest footballers Luke Farrell had ever played with or against. He had an abundance of natural talent coupled with an attitude and energy for the game that guaranteed success. Few people would argue with the claim that David had won the All-Ireland Cup Final against Stella Maris single-handedly. Football is a team game – fundamentally – but anyone at Tolka Park that sunny Sunday in June would testify to the mammoth display by the fifteen-year-old centre-half. He too had been rejected by Everton, but interest from another professional club and a second bite at the cherry seemed inevitable.

That is, until he walked out on the Stretford Enders in August. David had called into Barnes' Sports Store two hours before the start of pre-season training to tell Jerome he no longer wished to play for the team. Despite numerous attempts by both players and manager to talk him round, David had not kicked a ball in anger since. Luke, Copper Martin and Leslie Ward formed a diplomatic team and spent four hours the next evening trying to convince him to change his mind. No joy. Attempts to persuade him to reconsider his decision reached fever-pitch over the next fortnight. Phone calls, personal meetings, e-mails – everyone involved with the Stretford Enders worked themselves to exhaustion. Nothing changed.

David steadfastly refused to return.

At first, this led to rumours of a move to Home Farm, Stella Maris, Cherry Orchard or Lourdes Celtic – one of the traditional big guns of Dublin junior soccer and a better position in the shop window. But it all proved to be idle speculation. Not only did David walk out on the Enders. He walked out on football, full stop.

Luke was determined to find out why. He sat on the Dart, biting an index fingernail as the green carriages snaked along the coastline like a mechanical caterpillar. He had been thinking about this 'situation' for a while. David had become incredibly reclusive. He walked to school alone, disappeared at lunch time and stayed back for Junior Cert exam study time each evening. Copper Martin and fellow Enders Alan Giles and Edgar O'Lone had all tried to get inside his head. They had known David the longest and were his oldest set of friends. But their attempts to find out what was troubling him yielded little success. Leslie Ward, his cousin, had countless heart-to-hearts but always drew a blank on the million-dollar question: 'What's the matter?'

Luke decided it was time he took over the investigation. On the short bus journey from Dun Laoghaire to Baker's Corner he decided on a wonderful ploy to entice David out of his carefully constructed shell. When Michael Turner called to check on his progress, he would namedrop David as a prime candidate for a trial with Preston North End. Maybe this kind of attention could help rejuvenate his passion for football. It was a great idea. Even Luke felt a sense of excitement. The plan evolved in his mind. He would wave this bait in front of David – on the condition he rejoin the Enders and help them through the rocky period without their most influential player. Jerome could become involved and with any luck David would play with his usual polish and impress Michael Turner. In fact, by the time Luke returned to the fold and signed his contract with Preston, David Swayne would already be starring for their youth team.

There was a light drizzle falling when Luke stepped down off the 46A and began to hop towards Merrion Park estate. He was getting to grips with the crutches, more slowly than surely. What was normally a three-minute journey from bus stop to front door took twelve with the aid of crutches. Luke pressed the doorbell and waited patiently for an answer. It was almost a minute before it opened. He let out a groan when it did.

'What do you want?' Peter Swayne snapped.

'David,' Luke replied sharply.

'He's not in.' Swayne surveyed Luke's plaster cast with a gleeful smirk. He began a shrill chuckle, deciding to forgo his planned smart-arse remark.

Luke didn't have time to waste on wasters. 'Look, will he be back soon?' he said.

Swayne continued to chuckle. He wasn't in the mood to be helpful, polite or civil. Not to a sworn enemy.

'Swayne!' Luke said loudly. This infuriated Swayne. He stepped out of the porch and eyeballed his old adversary. He attempted to intimidate with his superior physical presence, but such psychological sway was no longer possible.

'Watch your mouth, Honchee,' Swayne hissed. 'Your hippy mate can't protect you now.'

Swayne was referring to Tonka, who was two hundred miles away in Liverpool training at Everton's youth academy. This fact did not worry Luke in the slightest. He straightened up and stood toe-to-toe. There was an obvious difference in height and weight, but an important point had been made. There was no fear.

'Tell David to call me as soon as he gets in. It's really important,' Luke said.

Swayne stood seething. 'Piss off,' he replied abruptly.

Luke decided to cut his losses. 'Never mind, I'll call him when I get home.'

Swayne remained outside the porch, his breath steaming off into the sky, reflecting his fierce sense of disgust. Luke hopped down Merrion Grove, occasionally glancing back at his former nightmare. It was pathetic, Peter Swayne. How the mighty had fallen.

Message in the Morning

Luke was desperate to find an alternative destination. He did have a quick poke about Champion Sports in the Bloomfield shopping centre, but in the end he conceded defeat and headed back to D'Argo's palace in Killiney. Martina would be waiting for him; the worst-case scenario was becoming cornered in his bedroom. If this happened, the TLC expended could be unbearable. To counter this eventuality, he spent as much time as possible in the living room. D'Argo was away on business – attending some conference at Lake Como, Italy, for organic food suppliers. Something to do with the advantages of wholesale shopping on the Internet. Boredom was curtailed with a game of *Championship Manager 01/02* on Martina's brand spanking new Fujitsu PC. Sustenance was provided by a chef's special chow mein from the Golden Gate Chinese takeaway. By half ten Everton were handily positioned in fourth place in the Premiership table. The shock of a fifth-round FA Cup defeat at the hands of lowly Port Vale was tempered by an up-coming appearance in the Worthington Cup Final against the might of Southampton. By midnight, Luke was exhausted. David Swayne didn't return any of his phone calls – his mobile was switched off. Luke rang his house three times over the course of Monday evening, leaving the same simple message with David's mother, but still no joy. The stubborn sod would need a personal visit and a good kick up the arse to bring him back into the world of the living. That was fine. At least it provided one stellar reason to leave the house on Tuesday.

It was impossible for Luke to sleep on in the mornings. From half six onwards his bedroom was engulfed in daylight. If that wasn't bad enough, the sound of the waves crashing onto the shore and the occasional seabird silhouette swooping past his curtains culminated in the most effective natural alarm clock known to man. He struggled out of bed and hobbled into his en suite loo. He let out a joyous sigh. The move from Montague Avenue to Killiney had filled him with fear. But unsteady as his position might be, the facilities in D'Argo's palace left anywhere else in the shade. Massive bedroom, spacious balcony with panoramic view. He could even see the Air Safety beacon, where he had slept rough some three months earlier.

It was an ironic twist of fate. A kid from the northside of Dublin ending up in the ivory towers of Killiney with the pop stars, supermodels, actors and F-1 drivers. How long he would remain in their company was a more tenuous affair. Luke understood the wonders and workings of the world in metaphors purely football. D'Argo wanted Martina. He was willing to spend an exorbitant amount of money to secure her services. Luke was the makeweight in the deal. Wim Jonk ended up at Inter Milan with Dennis Bergkamp in similar circumstances, signed because he was Bergkamp's best friend. Come to think of it, Luke was more like Jimmy 'Five Bellies' Gardner. When Gazza signed for Lazio in 1992, Five Bellies received a substantial wage from the club simply to keep him company.

'Morning,' Luke said as he hopped into the kitchen.

Martina was at the counter, buttering toast. 'Your

breakfast's on the table,' she replied.

Luke smiled. Maybe this TLC business did have a few positive points. Martina had done a sneaky fry-up. Sausages, rashers, pudding (black and white), waffles and a plate piled high with buttered toast.

'Not a word to Jonathan,' she said. She walked across with a second plate of toast. Luke mumbled something with his mouth full. She didn't scold him over manners. She was too busy taking a sly opportunity to kiss him on the crown.

'Thanks, Ma,' Luke said. He turned to watch her walk back to the kitchen counter and sip her coffee. This pact of silence was all part of a worrying series of events. After Mrs Hendy's death, D'Argo saw an opportunity to exploit, like all good businessmen. He offered Martina, and Luke, rent-free accommodation. He invited them to stay at his home indefinitely as guests. This generous offer came with no strings attached. No visible strings. But Luke had a different perspective to Martina.

No sooner had they arrived in his home than Jonathan passed on his vegetarian beliefs to her. The cooking and consumption of meat under his own roof turned his stomach. Luke had no intention of chomping lettuce and string beans. The following impasse meant D'Argo was faced with compromise number one. But men like him never sit easy with compromise. The concept is alien to them, and any deal they strike is always temporary. That word sent the occasional shiver down Luke's spine. It could easily be applied to his stay in Killiney.

Luke's attention was broken by the telephone ringing.

'I'll get it,' Martina said. Slowly, she tore her eyes from the IT textbook she had been studying and picked up the phone. 'Hello,' she said politely.

Luke turned to the fry-up. He had no interest in

earwigging on his mother's telephone conversations. Not when there were fried pieces of pig in front of him.

'Oh, Jesus.'

Luke turned sharply. Martina's quivering voice caught his attention. He watched in horror as she slumped to the side, stretching out her left hand to steady herself against the kitchen counter. Her face was shot of any colour or vitality: this was *bad* news. But who from?

'OK, Mo. Thanks for calling,' Martina said softly.

Luke's jaw dropped. Ella, something had happened to Ella. 'Ma?' he said anxiously.

Martina lifted her head. Two skinny streams of tears were running down her cheeks. She moved her right hand to her mouth and clamped her index finger between her teeth like a child sucking on a soother.

'Ma, what's wrong?' Luke said firmly.

Her eyes drifted to the kitchen window. She continued crying, unable to relay the news. Luke tried to stand up without the aid of his crutches. The blank moment of silence was tearing him apart.

'What's wrong?' he said loudly.

Martina snapped out of her daze. She stared at Luke carefully and composed herself. 'That was Mo Barnes,' she said.

Luke couldn't wait any longer. 'Yeah, what's wrong?' he prompted.

'It's David Swayne,' Martina replied.

Luke was surprised at the name. He was thinking only of Ella. What had David got to do with anything? Martina sobbed sadly, shaking her head in disbelief. She tried to compose herself, call up some reserve of strength, but she still quivered as she delivered the news.

'He's dead, Luke. He hanged himself last night.'

It took a good half-minute for the news to sink in. Then,

Luke calmly took his crutches and stood up. He hopped down the hall at a steady pace. Martina watched him go, but decided not to follow. Three minutes later, he returned to the kitchen fully dressed. He stared at his mother with a straight, sombre expression. She didn't know what to say, but it didn't matter. Words and phrases had no bearing on his state of mind. Verbal counselling would have no effect. He took his rain jacket from the coat hanger and unbolted the front door.

'I'll be on the beach,' Luke said calmly.

Martina nodded her head. 'OK.'

They stared at one another a while. Luke sensed his mother was awaiting his approval for a physical embrace. In truth she needed it more than him. He opened his arms, urging her forward. Martina settled her head against her son's chest and cried the tears of a mother. Three miles away, another mother was facing up to life without her child. A pain that could never be erased.

Clear skies reigned overhead. Luke sat on the pebbly beach, staring up at the sky in that listless way people do when their mind is dealing with immense emotion. David Swayne had taken his own life.

The notion that life had become so unbearable for David that the only solution was suicide filled Luke with a sense of guilt and shame he never thought he would feel again. He could hear the creepy whisper of the Air Safety beacon behind him, the barely audible blimp of the red light bulb atop the pole. Three months earlier he had spent a night sleeping rough in Dalkey quarry, after going into a self-styled exile from his family and friends. David Swayne had paid him a visit that night with a bottle of vodka wrapped in a brown paper bag.

Luke recalled the words David had said to him: 'You've no idea what a real problem is . . .'

David was screaming out for help. But all Luke could think about back then was his own meagre concerns. Everton, Ella, D'Argo – pointless crap that made no difference in the grand scheme of things. He thought about last Saturday afternoon in St James's Hospital. He and Jerome crying like babies over a stupid game. Football mattered more to him than his friends. All that time in the summer after Everton turned David down; in the autumn when he walked out on the Enders and shut himself off from the rest of the world; all that time when he was silently screaming out for a friend, someone to help him find a reason to go on living.

What did Luke worry about? Himself and his precious football career. A game that lasts ninety minutes and then ends with the shrill squeal of a whistle. It would never amount to life and death, no matter how much you argued to the contrary. It was nothing more than a game. He employed both his crutches and gradually clawed his way onto his feet. The throbbing pain in his leg barely affected his concentration. He stared out at the calm sea.

'It's all my fault,' he said softly. There was no one around to argue to the contrary. That suited Luke fine. The judge and jury had been his mind and conscience. There was no more fair and impartial deliberator than yourself.

The Funeral

Sometime between half ten and half eleven on the evening of Monday 4 November, David Swayne kicked away the chair beneath his feet and swung from the centre beam in his garden shed. The noose on his father's brown leather belt tightened around his throat and minutes later he was dead. It was the report filed by the coroner before releasing the body for burial. A full week and a day later, a massive congregation packed inside St Joseph's church, opposite Woodlawn Comprehensive, to pay their final respects to a popular and well-respected young man. Luke sat in the fifth row from the front with Ella, Tonka and the rest of 5C. The whole school turned out in their uniforms, wearing black armbands as a mark of respect.

'I've asked those who knew David best to say some words,' Father O'Connor said.

Leslie Ward made his way to the pulpit to read a prepared speech. He broke down on four separate occasions, but with the help of Father O'Connor made it to the end. Copper Martin was next. His voice was calm and peaceful, but his words managed to squeeze a tear from the driest eye.

'I'll never stop thinking about you, David,' he said softly. 'I don't think it's possible to forget someone like you.'

Ella was deeply touched by his words. She turned to Luke for a comforting hug. He held her in his arms, wiping the tears from her cheek. Inside, every time someone mentioned

David's name, guilt formed an acidic compound in his gut and squeezed his insides tight.

In essence, Luke was embroiled in his own personal hell. But instead of skulking off to a corner to bemoan his misfortune, he resolved to open his heart and comfort those around him. He glanced over Ella's shoulder to Tonka. He sat rigid in his Everton tracksuit, sporting a freshly shorn crew-cut. He stared right back at Luke, his eyes glazing over. In fact, the entire congregation was awash with tears. Even the most granite, po-faced characters were sobbing like little children. Mr Duffy, 5C's hard-boiled tutor, wore the expression of a tiny toddler, searching desperately for his mummy in a large department store.

Luke possessed the only set of dry eyes in the church. And not for the want of trying. He felt like a farmer in a desert region, praying for rain to no avail. The rot and decay of his inner being was dishing out punishment in the worst way possible.

'It's all right to cry, Luke,' Ella whispered. He focused on her. She wiped away the latest wave of tears to saturate her cheeks with a baby-blue hankie. Luke felt a build-up of pressure around him. She was waiting for a reaction he could not produce. Soon enough, the world would recognise his callous inadequacy.

'I know,' Luke replied. He turned away, searching the landscape of the church interior for something to focus on. He found it. In the front row, Peter Swayne sat to the left of his parents with Cecilia Giles, his sometime girlfriend, in tow. Luke watched carefully. Swayne shared his inability. Not a trace of liquid grief upon his face.

'Jerome Barnes will now say some words,' Father O'Connor announced.

Luke felt he should pay close attention to the eulogy. But

his fascination with Peter Swayne was powerful. Only the distressing amplified sound of Jerome gasping for air broke the spell. Luke melted into the mass of eyes and ears watching the manager of the Stretford Enders. He took a long look about the faces packed inside the church before speaking.

'I have this speech,' Jerome said, displaying the white pages as proof. 'But, I . . . I don't think it'll do David justice.'

Jerome stopped and attempted to compose his thoughts. The tears were already flowing, true to his emotional nature. He glanced at the brown coffin, draped with David's favourite red Liverpool jersey.

'We all knew David, didn't we?' he sobbed.

The congregation was still.

'I don't need to tell you about him. You all knew him, he was David Swayne. That's all we need to know. That's why this church is bursting at the seams.'

It was the most beautiful, heartfelt eulogy anyone could ever deliver. Even Father O'Connor had to wipe a tear from his eye.

'Look at us,' Jerome said quietly. 'Look at each other's faces.'

His suggestion captured the mood perfectly. People turned to one another, husbands to wives, fathers to mothers, sons to daughters, brothers to sisters, cousins to aunts, uncles to nieces, nephews to friends. Everyone in the church made themselves aware of the surrounding grief and sorrow.

' "We" say it all,' Jerome said gently. Moments later, he stepped down from the altar, stopping briefly to gently caress the coffin. The sight of him breaking down once more had a domino effect. The chain reaction brought the service to a standstill, people weeping profusely. Everyone, it seemed, apart from Luke . . . and Peter Swayne.

* * *

The majority of the mourners who sat in St Joseph's church followed on to Deansgrange cemetery. A steady procession laid wreaths at the feet of the Swayne family, headed by a broken-hearted father and mother. Jack and Zoë Swayne were a respectable middle-class couple from Stillorgan. A senior solicitor and a faithful housewife with two handsome teenage sons. Their idyllic lifestyle with its semi-detached home in an upwardly mobile neighbourhood, the two-car family and the sophisticated foreign holidays had been shattered by suicide.

Luke, Ella, Tonka and the other Enders stood some twenty yards back from the grave. Luke watched the movements of the family carefully. David had been the spitting image of his father, who stood tall and proud in a full-length black cashmere coat, thanking the wreath-layers for their kindness. He threw a comforting arm around his wife's shoulder as the coffin was slowly lowered into the damp, cold earth. Standing beside his parents was Peter Swayne. He was still to shed a tear. Somehow, Luke found this comforting. He despised his ability to plunder such a selfish emotion from tragedy, but he could sense a similarity between Swayne's state of mind and his own. All the telltale signs of guilt were written across his face. The pallid complexion, the empty, elsewhere expression, the slow-motion reflexes. Perhaps the same infestation that was consuming Luke from the inside was at work on Swayne.

Ella gripped Luke's left arm. 'Are you ready?' she said softly.

Luke turned to her. He noticed the quiet passing of the mourners. Father O'Connor walked by with the funeral directors and some teachers from Woodlawn Comprehensive. It was time to go.

'Luke, are you OK?' Tonka said kindly.

It took him a moment to gather his bearings. He noticed Jerome, Mo, Martina and D'Argo walking amongst a group of parents. Tonka and Ella waited on Luke's reply anxiously.

'Luke,' Ella said. She massaged some feeling back into his arm. He placed his hand on top of hers, then stared into Tonka's eyes with a renewed strength.

'I want to wait a while,' he said calmly. It seemed a reasonable request. Tonka went off with the other Enders while Ella stayed by his side and turned back to look at the grave. The only people who remained by the gaping hole in the ground were the immediate family and, a few yards further back, the grave diggers.

'I can't believe he's gone,' Ella said sadly.

Luke wasn't paying attention. 'Yeah,' he replied vacantly.

A few minutes later, Jack and Zoë Swayne departed the graveside, surrounded on all sides by their family. Luke and Ella stood back to let them pass onto the rugged path. Ella bowed her head respectfully. When they were gone, Luke looked back at the grave. He watched the grave diggers move in. There were two more people yet to leave. Peter Swayne stared into the hole at the coffin covered with wreaths and tiny balls of muck. Cecilia Giles was by his side, her arms folded. It would be fair to say she didn't look too upset. This theory was backed up by her hasty departure. She and Peter had a brief verbal exchange before she left. What a wonderful girlfriend.

Cecilia passed by Ella and Luke without a word. Ella attempted to say hello, but received no reply. It annoyed her, but she let it pass.

'Perhaps she's not a funeral person,' Ella said dryly.

Luke made no attempt to answer. Peter Swayne was becoming a more captivating sight with each passing moment. He studied the expression on his face with great care. The pain was evident for all to see. It reminded him of someone not a million miles away.

'Luke,' Ella said. This time she gently tugged his arm and turned his body until he faced her. Luke blinked his eyes like someone awakening from stasis.

'I think it's time to go,' she said softly. Luke stared into her eyes. They shared a slow, tender kiss on the lips before walking from the cemetery. He did manage a parting glance at Swayne, who stood like a stone statue and seemed to have no intention of leaving the graveside anytime soon. The diggers worked around him.

Up ahead of Luke and Ella, Cecilia Giles had stopped at the gates of the cemetery to enjoy a Marlboro Light with a small man decked out in matching denim jacket and jeans. His hair was black, curly and greasy, his skin olive coloured and his chin adorned with a precision-cut goatee beard. Slung from his left shoulder was a small, chunky black bag with the word CANON written in white along the strap.

'Oh, hello,' Cecilia said with a chirpy smile as Luke and Ella passed by. The two-faced nature of her greeting was scandalous. Ella smiled in reply, not wanting to appear ignorant on today of all days. But after walking a short distance out of earshot she had to comment.

'Do you think she took lessons?' she said.

'In what?' Luke replied.

'Ignorance.'

THE END OF ERAS

Some traditions are blind to the mood of the modern age. The teenagers from Woodlawn Comprehensive invited back to the Melting Pot pub off the Stillorgan dual carriageway for a drink and a sandwich felt awkward at the thought of consuming food or alcohol. The Swayne family sat in the lounge, quietly toasting the passing of one of their clan with the same sense of dignity and pride as they had done for generations.

But this was no ordinary funeral.

'I can't take this,' Luke said to Tonka quietly. The Enders and 5C were bunched at the bar, quietly munching ham and cheese sandwiches. All except Luke, who took to his crutches and hopped out into the beer garden. A biting November breeze blew across the concrete courtyard. It was ten past three in the afternoon and the fading daylight up above did little to lift the spirit.

'Luke,' a voice said. Tonka closed the bar door behind him and slid in alongside Luke at the first wooden picnic table. He smiled, trying to lighten the depressing mood.

'I can't stand it, Tonk,' Luke explained. 'Sitting there, staring into space. Trying to think of something to say.'

Tonka nodded. The emotional cauldron of the church and cemetery had passed. The pause was over – life had officially restarted. David, no matter how much people loved him, would inevitably become a memory.

'That's the way things are,' Tonka said.

Luke turned sharply to face him. This was not some early cup exit for Everton. This was not about Ireland failing to qualify for the World Cup Finals. David Swayne was dead. One of their best friends was gone for ever.

'What's that supposed to mean?' Luke said angrily.

Tonka stood his ground. 'David's gone,' he replied coldly.

Luke was outraged. He sat seething with anger, aiming this vitriol squarely at the callous remarks of Tonka Matthews. In reality, he was boiling over with self-loathing. It was the bitter sensation of jealousy at the sight and sound of a clear conscience; the ease and peace of mind in which Tonka was able to grieve his lost friend. He had been in Liverpool, but if he'd been in Dublin, he would have made a difference. Maybe if Luke had been picked for the youth academy and Tonka had stayed behind David Swayne would be alive and well. He would still be playing for the Enders and life would go on as normal. Luke's planned attack fell to pieces. He gasped in a breath before turning away from Tonka, unable to look such a selfless do-gooder in the eye. Seconds later he felt a giant hand on his shoulder.

'Luke,' Tonka said.

Luke had the courtesy to face him.

'I loved David,' Tonka went on quietly. It was a sweet moment. Tonka wasn't great with words. He didn't have the command of a vast vocabulary to start listing reasons or reminiscing in depth about the good times they shared together. All he possessed within his limited sphere of expression was sincerity. 'And I'll never forget him,' he concluded.

Luke opened up his arms again. He and Tonka Matthews embraced. It was a special moment, but for differing reasons. Tonka felt a sense of liberty. The pain was purged from his soul. He could now face the world once more. But each time Luke had embraced a friend or loved one, which was frequently over the past seven days, he felt another piece of his insides crumble to dust. Each embrace bore a hole in his heart.

'Pre-season was torture,' Tonka said. 'They run you into the ground.'

'What about the matches?' Luke said.

'The B matches are OK. You can live with the pace. But the A games are unreal. The competition is something fierce.'

Luke studied Tonka carefully as he talked. The new haircut wasn't the only change. Somehow, he seemed to have grown up over the past three months. He appeared more relaxed in the presence of others. Making the grade as a professional footballer had cracked the loner shell in two. A confident smile replaced the trademark sombre frown.

'. . . Oh, by the way, Stacy asked me to get your new address,' Tonka said.

This revelation knocked Luke clean out of observation mode. 'What?' he replied, after a period of delayed shock.

'She never stops talking about you. Luke this, Luke that. You hung her out to dry,' Tonka said.

Luke gave a nervous glance into the bar to check on the whereabouts of Ella. Stacy Culshaw was still a sensitive topic of conversation in these parts. Something and someone which had not been mentioned since July.

'Look, say I've emigrated to Australia or something,' Luke said discreetly.

Tonka shook his head. 'No way, Rico. She's well wide of that kind of stunt. The boss and Terry are on the phone to each other every week. She's kept right up to date on your progress.'

Luke thought about it momentarily. It was quite flattering to have someone holding a candle. He smiled briefly, then turned to Tonka with a cheeky suggestion. 'Does she know about Preston?' he said.

Tonka nodded emphatically. It was his turn to check on Ella's position. He leaned close to Luke's ear and whispered. 'I think that's part of her master plan,' he said.

'What is?' Luke replied.

Tonka spelt it out. 'You, Preston, April, medical.'

Luke stared at him. He tipped his nostril with an index finger. That was all the information he was willing to divulge. Before Luke could come back with a second line of questioning, the bar door opened.

'Hello,' a familiar voice said. Cecilia Giles stepped out onto the concrete slabs of the freezing courtyard. Luke and Tonka stared at her in confusion. It was more than a year since she and Luke had been involved in a conversation with one another, civil or otherwise. As for Tonka and Cecilia, they had never spoken directly to one another in their lives.

'Belated congratulations,' Cecilia said.

Tonka glanced at Luke momentarily. 'Oh, erm, thanks,' he replied.

In the year following her humiliation on or, more precisely, off the stage of *Star Search*, Cecilia Giles had come up in the world, quite literally. She was now a scratch under six foot tall and had blossomed into a truly stunning specimen. The automatic sidestep from her failed attempt at pop stardom was the fashion world. In this, she found her true calling in life. She signed to the Image Inc. modelling agency at the age of fifteen and had been inundated with work ever since. Her natural good looks, excellent posture, sleek, slender physique, never-ending legs and wide arsenal of moody facial expressions made her the darling of the Irish fashion world.

'I would *love* to come and see you play sometime,' Cecilia said softly.

Luke watched her move closer to Tonka in her classically seductive manner. Déjà vu was running rife in his mind. It was an act as old as the pyramids.

'Well, I'm on standby for the Ireland under-eighteen squad for the match against England,' Tonka said awkwardly. 'It's on at Tolka Park.'

Cecilia stared deeply into his eyes. She was one of the few girls who could do this without running the risk of a strained neck. As the sordid little scene played out, Luke felt the heaving of his insides go into overdrive. The fact that they had buried a close friend hours earlier seemed lost on the lusting pair. Cecilia took a small fuchsia calling card from her handbag and handed it to Tonka.

'What size boots do you wear?' she said softly.

Tonka gulped nervously. 'Erm, size twelve,' he replied.

Cecilia's eyes sparkled. 'Call me the next time you're in town,' she said.

'What's your game?' Luke said, interrupting.

Cecilia waited a while before turning to answer him. 'Excuse me?' she said.

Luke gasped in disbelief. ' "Excuse me?" . . . I don't know if you've been paying attention at all today, but we just buried your boyfriend's little brother,' he said bitterly.

Cecilia seemed unmoved. Before turning to depart she left Tonka with a long, luscious stare to remember her by. It was a sickening act, something far beyond reproach. When the bar door closed, Luke turned to his friend, expecting nothing less than the card torn into tiny pieces. That was

Tonka, he had character. But to his deepening disgust, there was no discernible action.

Luke had to prompt him. 'Well?' he said.

Tonka sat silent. He didn't have to say a single word. Luke was fast becoming an expert at spotting guilt and shame in mere expressions. The young footballer was parading both emotions like fifty-foot billboard posters. This was the final straw.

'I'll see you around,' Luke said.

Tonka wanted to call after him. But his sense of shame rendered him mute. Luke struggled up from his seat and hopped back inside the bar. He immediately started to look for Ella. He needed to escape the madness of the Melting Pot. There was only one place left to seek solace.

'Ella,' Luke said, interrupting a 5C class conversation. He gestured for her to join him. She moved past the assembled throng to his side.

'What's the matter?' she said.

'Can we go somewhere? I have to get out of here,' Luke replied, the upset in his voice plain to hear.

Ella massaged his arm and looked at him kindly. 'Yeah, course. I'll just get me jacket,' she said.

Luke waited by the bar for her to return. He noticed the door to the beer garden open once more. Tonka stepped back into the bar and stared at him shame-faced. He couldn't maintain eye contact and bowed his head. Luke decided to save him the bother and turned one hundred eighty degrees to find a new focus of attention. As luck would have it, Cecilia and Peter Swayne were standing on the other side of the bar, directly facing Tonka. Cecilia chatted with her denim-clad photographer friend from the cemetery gates. Peter seemed to be on the periphery of the conversation. Not that he looked too bothered. His eyes were distant and bleak.

Luke guessed his thoughts were in a similar, removed location.

'Luke, long time no see,' a voice said from behind.

Luke closed his eyes and swallowed a groan. He prepared his most stomach-churning fake smile. 'All right, Wes?' he said quietly, turning to greet the grinning buffoon.

'Sorry to hear about your little accident,' Weasel said, completely missing the turn-off sign for tact. 'Still, them's the breaks,' he added, with an irritating snigger.

Luke was never really in the right frame of mind to deal with Weasel Adams. But today of all days, his ability to feign tolerance was dangerously low.

'Hey, Luke, you missed a great gig last Saturday,' Weasel continued.

Luke took a deep breath. Weasel was winding him up now. It was obvious.

'Not to worry, plenty more gigs to come,' Luke said.

Weasel sipped his vodka blackcurrant and shrugged his shoulders. 'I suppose,' he murmured.

Luke glanced across the bar. He could see Ella standing with Jerome, Mo and Martina at the parents' table. They were involved in a deep discussion. It didn't look anything like end-of-conversation time, meaning he would have to put up with the most obnoxious prick on God's green earth a little while longer.

'Oh, by the way, Luke, I don't suppose Ella mentioned the duet,' Weasel said.

Luke faced him. 'No, she didn't,' he replied curtly.

'Yeah, "Back to Love". We played it at the showcase gig in London last week. The people at Fab Note insisted it go on the album,' Weasel explained.

'Really?' Luke said, fighting desperately hard not to take the bait.

'Yes, well. They were anxious I take a more . . .

"hands-on" role with Ella . . . and the Starfish,' Weasel said, smirking from cheek to cheek.

Luke stared his foe down. The battle lines were clearly drawn. 'Back to Love', a single from the Brand New Heavies' album *Brother, Sister*, was the tune he and Ella had listened to when they first sat in her bedroom, as a couple, learning how to kiss. This proposed duet represented an attack on the most ancient artefact of their relationship and – in Luke's mind – the most sacred. Weasel Adams was growing braver and bolder with each passing month. His constant taunting and needling was a tactic born out of the summer break-up. The first sign of a split between Luke and Ella gave him just the kind of motivation he needed to drive them apart for ever.

'Hi,' Ella said, linking Luke's left arm. Luke noticed Jerome by her side. He was holding a brown envelope and looking straight at him.

'Read this,' he said, handing the envelope to Luke. 'Give us a call when you've done,' he added.

Luke looked up at Jerome, slightly bemused by the exchange. There was no clue given away in his manager's facial expression.

Jerome turned and headed back to the other parents in the lounge. Weasel observed the happy couple with the conniving countenance of a master saboteur. He threw a new monkey-wrench in the works.

'I was just telling Luke about the duet,' Weasel said.

Luke was on the verge of violence. 'I'll wait for you outside,' he said to Ella, still staring viciously at Weasel.

He didn't pay attention when she called out his name. He hopped straight from the bar. Along the way, he noticed Tonka seated in a booth, surrounded by a legion of starstruck Enders. Although clearly aware of his presence, he was unable to look Luke in the eye. Cecilia and her photographer friend were stationed at the far end of the bar, still locked in debate. Peter Swayne was nowhere to be seen. It was a funny feeling, but as he made his way outside the Melting Pot, Luke actually felt sorry for him, something unthinkable eight days before. It just went to show. What a weird world.

Luke managed to calm down after his run-in with Weasel Adams. He and Ella walked the short distance from the Melting Pot to Monkstown Dart station. The chilly sea breeze blew the cobwebs off them, after the stuffy, smoky atmosphere of the bar. The Dart brought them six stops down the line to Killiney, and ten minutes later they opened the front door of D'Argo's palace.

'What a day,' Ella said quietly.

Luke didn't reply. He was busy punching the security code into the keypad to disable the alarm system. He had a rotten head for numbers and needed total concentration to enter the six-digit code correctly.

'Will I turn the lights on?' Ella said.

'Yeah,' Luke replied, after finishing with the keypad. His diligent attention to the alarm system was the direct result of an unfortunate mishap a few days after he and Martina moved into D'Argo's palace. Luke punched in the wrong code one morning after popping out to the local shop and had to listen to the ear-piercing siren for half an hour. Eventually, he called Martina at work, but before she could return home to turn the system off a Garda car rolled past and the officers came inside to investigate. They found Luke and, upon hearing his accent, placed him under arrest, despite the fact that he possessed a set of keys. Martina arrived ten minutes later and set about the officers for hassling her son. Result? She was placed under arrest. Only when an extremely embarrassed D'Argo rushed home from a board meeting would the police accept the story peddled by Martina and Luke.

Talk about getting off on the wrong foot.

Since that day, Luke was determined to live the life of a church mouse. That included tolerable TV and stereo volumes, neat and mannerly food consumption and the placement of all school books, kit bags and dirty boxer shorts out of sight of his gracious landlord.

'Can I get a drink?' Ella said, having illuminated the hall and kitchen.

'Yeah, get me something too,' Luke replied.

'A please would be nice,' Ella said as she walked over to the fridge.

'Please,' Luke added without fuss.

Ella took out two cans of Coke and followed Luke, who headed straight for his bedroom. He turned on his father's record player and decided to go with the peace, love and understanding of Stevie Wonder and *Songs in the Key of Life*, Volume One. Ella was making herself comfortable on his bed and he moved to join her. He laid his crutches on the floor and slid on beside her. They faced one another and kissed tenderly. Ever since they left the Melting Pot, Luke had been meaning to tell Ella that he loved her. It crossed his mind that saying the actual words once in a while showed how much he cared.

But before he could squeeze out those three little words, Ella cut him off.

'I need to tell you something,' she said. There was that voice again. The chance of this being good news was Jodie Kidd slim. Luke braced himself for heartache.

'While we were in London, the CEO of Fab Note made a

'suggestion,' she said softly. It was a pretty vague opening. Luke declined the opportunity to intervene.

'Myself and the lads talked it through, and we've decided . . .'

Ella wanted him to ask her. This was blatantly obvious. But Luke didn't want to. He wanted to get his hands on one of those silver mind-ray thingies from *Men in Black* and zap this whole conversation out of existence.

'Decided what?' he said finally.

Ella had something cumbersome lodged at the bottom of her throat. This was a momentous piece of news, whatever it was. Luke found himself drawing away from her, ever so slightly.

'We're moving to London,' she said.

'What?'

'They want us in London for a year so we can write, record and showcase the first album.'

Ella smiled. This expression was a clear indication that the decision wasn't much of a wrench. Luke had been jettisoned from the mix without the emotional turmoil you would expect from any half-decent soap opera. To be fair, leaving Dublin to further her career was something of an in-evitability. London and Fab Note records had come calling – what else could she say? If Luke's leg wasn't encased in plaster, he would have signed the two-year contract and left for Preston the very next day. The disappointment in his eyes wasn't to do with her decision. It was all about his own sense of failure. Tonka had done it, Ella and the Funky Starfish had done it, but once more he had missed the boat.

'Luke, what do you think?' Ella said quietly, having waited a full minute for some sort of verbal reaction.

Luke looked up at her. He smiled, semi-sincerely. 'I think it's great,' he said.

Ella smiled. 'This won't change things between us. I'll call you every night. You can come over and visit.'

'Yeah, we'll work something out,' Luke replied cheerfully. He didn't believe a word of it. Ella moved forward and kissed him on the lips. Luke responded passionately. Already the image of the egg-timer was ripe in his mind. Time was now marked in a specific quantity and was fast running out.

Ella spent the night in Luke's bedroom. While she slept, her head nestled peacefully on his chest, he mulled the options over in his mind. There was a real danger that any decision he made would resemble another one of his trademark snap judgements. But on this occasion, he utilised a sensible period of time to weigh up the various pros and cons of the situation. A year was a long time in anyone's language, but Ella's ability to be faithful wasn't in question. After all, his paranoia that summer about her relationship with Weasel Adams had proved completely unfounded. It had turned out to be an elaborate fiction created by his jealous mind. And even when he used mere suspicion to justify his decision to cheat with Stacy Culshaw in Liverpool, Ella took this savage blow on the chin. She forgave Luke for his bout of summer insanity and never once threw it back in his face. It was this immense act of dignity and bravery under fire that emphasised her impeccable character.

But the one thing troubling Luke, the single detail boring away at his sense of pride, was the resentment Ella would start to feel after a full year of enforced celibacy. She was a human being, flesh and blood. Temptation would not be a problem to someone of her character, but what of loneliness, what of despair? The music industry was renowned as a party trade – gigs, press launches, record company-sponsored nights on the town. A week would be bearable, a month an acceptable struggle. But twelve months spurning the advances and invitations of handsome young men? Ella was sixteen years of age; this was the spring of her life and a unique opportunity.

Luke came to a conclusion.

Wednesday passed by in a blur. There was breakfast with Martina and D'Argo. A full day of packing in Sycamore Street and a bon voyage family meal to send the two Barnes children off into the big, bad world. At quarter past seven, Luke, Mo and Jerome prepared their final goodbyes outside the departure lounge in Dublin International Airport. Mo was a predictable monsoon of tears as her babies prepared to fly the coop. Jerome was strangely reserved and understated. Luke felt certain David's death was dominating his heart and mind.

'Well, kids, we'd better get a move on,' Weasel Adams announced happily. He unlocked Ella and Mo from their mother–daughter clench, lending his body as a wedge to pry them apart. He slung his arm around Mo's shoulder and gripped her tight to his chest.

'Don't worry, Mum, I'll look after her,' he promised, all the time staring at Luke. A vicious snarl in reply would give Weasel an unadulterated jolt of pleasure. Luke had no intention of squandering any more of his blood, sweat or tears for the swine's amusement.

'Take care, our kid,' Isaac said to Luke, embracing him with a loving hug.

Luke stood there and managed to say, 'Good luck,' but was unable to reciprocate the hug for fear of beheading one of the Starfish or an innocent passer-by with a flying crutch. The Funky Starfish disappeared down the tunnel to the departure lounge. Weasel Adams wanted to stay, but sensed Ella's need for privacy. Hanging about for no apparent reason could expose his hand. He decided to be patient, reflecting on the vast twelve-month period he had to make his final move. Jerome and Mo stood back to give the young couple the spotlight. Ella smiled: despite the flood of tears falling from her eyes, she felt happy and excited.

Luke had to do it now. 'I've decided to do this now . . . for both of us,' he said sadly.

Luke detached the repaired friendship bracelet from his right wrist and handed it to Ella. She stared past his pupils, not quite sure if this was for real or some kind of macabre joke. It was the passage of time allowed to pass without a word that sealed their fate.

This left Ella speechless.

'A year's a long time. Who knows where we'll be . . . how we'll feel,' Luke explained. He had chosen his moment well. The tannoy announced a final call for passengers on the eight o'clock flight to Heathrow Airport to board the plane. Ella could hardly argue the toss. Luke moved in closer and kissed her on the lips. All the feeling and passion passed in one direction. This wasn't a deliberate snub. The truth was, Ella was paralysed with shock. With the return of sensation to her limbs, she picked up her sky-blue leather holdall. She took one long last look at her ex-boyfriend before turning and walking through to the departure lounge.

Luke waited for her to disappear from his field of vision before turning to join Jerome and Mo. Nobody talked on the journey home to Sycamore Street, each person for a completely different reason.

Luke reached D'Argo's palace in Killiney a shade before nine o'clock. No one was home to greet him. A note on the kitchen counter detailed a last-minute charity function for the Irish Cancer Trust in the Herbert Park Hotel that

D'Argo, as president, and Martina, as his stunning girl-friend, had to attend.

Luke wasn't too bothered. He made a stop-start tour of the kitchen. The cupboard beside the oven for a family-size bag of tortilla chips. The fridge for a jar of spicy salsa dip, a two-litre bottle of Fanta and a white Magnum ice-cream bar. From the cupboard above the sink he retrieved a kilo bag of KP dry roasted peanuts, and finally, the portable telephone and the menu for Apache Pizza from the kitchen table. He turned his bedside lamp on and dialled the number. He ordered a sixteen-inch pepperoni and mushroom with a side order of chicken wings. While waiting for the scheduled twenty-five delivery minutes to elapse he relaxed on his bed.

Bad move.

The detectable scent of Ella's Polo Sport perfume filled his lungs with a foul-stenching gasp of regret. He could feel the parlour of unhappiness creak its doors open ever so slightly. David, Tonka, Mrs Hendy, Ronald and now Ella. All gone from his life.

In there somewhere was one body-blow too many.

Something beneath Luke's left shoulder blade was causing him considerable discomfort. He rolled onto his side and dug a hand beneath his duvet to find out what was adding to his list of woes. A brown A4 envelope. It didn't take long to figure out it came from Jerome. Luke had taken it from his manager before he and Ella left the Melting Pot after David's funeral. Now it offered some slight fascination, until his pizza arrived. He opened up the envelope and poured out the contents. A set of green-coloured sheets and a set of red-coloured sheets.

'Diet plan, exercise plan,' Luke said in surprise.

It seemed Jerome had designed a programme for Luke to retain his fitness while his leg was in plaster. It included upper body exercises and a special workout routine for people without the use of a limb or limbs. That seemed fair enough. But the diet sheet included a list of meals, breakfast, lunch and dinner, sorely lacking in sugar, salt and all-round snack content.

Luke was in no mood to consider his health. Jerome's plan received due attention. The red sheets scattered somewhere behind the radiator while the green sheets landed as a united party in the bottom drawer of his computer table.

Days in Decline

It was simple really. With Ella gone, Luke allowed his life to suddenly collapse into a dark, hollow chasm that amounted to nothing. No friends, no romance, no football. Even the simple pleasures provided by an hour-long jaunt up and down the coast on board a Dart or an evening stroll along Killiney beach had become logistical nightmares with his right leg caked in plaster and the steep hike to and from Killiney train station. Stranded alone in D'Argo's palace on top of the hill like a latterday Rapunzel, he turned to the one-on-one comforts available within the confines of his luxurious prison to battle the sharp tongues of loneliness and despair. Sky Digital, PlayStation 2, the Internet and an endless procession of junk food.

Martina no longer had the burden of a monthly rent bill. With this mighty shackle removed from their lives, her ever-increasing income was available for far more frivolous investment. The two or three requests Luke made each week for takeaway dinner funds seemed more reasonable. It was hideously ironic. Locked up in the luxury home of a health-food millionaire, Luke proceeded to gorge his way from a lean and muscular ten-stone frame to a flabby twelve three. He just could not stop eating. Five or six nights a week minimum, both D'Argo and his mother would be engaged with work or study until ten or eleven p.m.

D'Argo's business seemed to be expanding by the day,

hence he was always called away for meetings, conferences, etc. etc. Martina was in the third year of her information technology degree. The added responsibility of her position as junior stock-controller for Boots Ireland kept her occupied Monday to Friday eight a.m. till eleven p.m., more often than not. Whatever time remained, remained for sleep. This ready-made veil of privacy allowed Luke to stuff his face without the prying eyes or silent facial accusations that might have triggered a modicum of guilt or shame in his mind. It was too easy to blame his shocking thirty-pound weight gain on Martina and D'Argo. But the guilt-free vacuum they unwittingly constructed around him wasn't helpful.

Of course, Luke could not plead complete alienation. Others tried to help him – one person in particular. But he was operating in a world of denial. He skilfully sidestepped the issue of his weight gain in the same way he would side-step an opposing defender. By the middle of December the alarming routine of gluttony he had effortlessly slipped into was something far more damaging to his blossoming football career than the broken shinbone he had suffered in October.

The routine.

Breakfast would start at Dun Laoghaire Dart station. Two king-size Snickers bars, a packet of king-size Rancheros and a bag of KP dry roasted to keep him ticking over till lunch time. At the stroke of one, Luke made a lonely bee-line for Macari's chipper on Woodlawn Avenue. Two large singles, two battered sausages, a quarter-pounder with cheese and occasionally a bag of onion rings. Dinner consisted of vegetables and freshly cooked meat three nights a week, frozen bounty or takeaway upon the remaining four. It all amounted to isolation. He wasn't a couch potato by choice. He was rarely inside the house when fit and able. But a leg in plaster limited his range of activities. Sky Digital provided premium movies and sport. PlayStation 2 provided pure escapism. Internet chat rooms and an on-going e-mail friendship with Ronald helped him retain some shred of a stake in reality and the world outside his patio door. But the influence of all three shrank to microscopic levels when it came to food. This was the ultimate escapism. And more than that, food brought Luke pleasure. It was the one thing left in his life he could control. It was the perfect companion, there whenever he called. Food filled the protracted silences once occupied by friends and family.

Food was all Luke had left.

Ready to Return?

It didn't seem like three months since the accident. Luke found it hard to believe that in three short hours he would be able to stand on his own two feet. The appointment with Dr Singh in St James's Hospital was for six o'clock.

'Luke,' Martina called from the kitchen.

'Yeah, I'm coming,' he replied automatically.

It was nervous tension on his mother's part. Today would be her first venture into the city centre as a fully licensed driver. It was also the first time she would drive D'Argo's Cherokee Jeep without him by her side. The pressure was mounting. She paced the kitchen floor, glancing from hall to watch. Her plan to miss any hint of rush-hour traffic on the journey into the city centre relied on them leaving Killiney in the next fifteen minutes, just to be on the safe side.

'What's taking so long?' she groaned anxiously.

She walked down the hall to investigate Luke's snail-like pace in readying himself for the off. His bedroom door was open slightly, allowing her an insight that shocked and disturbed her. Since November, Luke had been attending school and walking round the house wearing various numbers from his vast selection of tracksuit bottoms. Today, he had decided to wear wide-leg jeans. With one small problem. The plethora of thirty-inch-waist denims no longer slipped snugly round his hips.

Martina gasped in despair as she watched her baby grunt and puff to fasten the buttons on his indigo Levi's shut. At that moment, her role in the neglect became apparent. Luke's trim physique, fashioned by a healthy combination of genetics and rigorous physical activity, was buried beneath three distinct rolls of flab. After a further thirty seconds of struggle, he conceded defeat and unbuttoned his jeans. He turned to the full-length mirror on his Sliderobe and glanced at the product of three months' comfort eating.

Martina was still outside the door, debating whether to intervene and offer a hug. It was painfully hard to just walk away as if nothing were wrong. But her action towards the matter in hand would have to be conducted with subtlety and sensitivity. She decided to bide her time and returned to the kitchen. Meanwhile, Luke had given up on snaking inside any material without an elasticised waist. He dressed in his new Everton tracksuit and prepared to leave his bedroom. Before going, he pulled out the contract Michael Turner had given to him in October and stared at the front page. Somehow, it still didn't seem real – the mess he had eaten his way into – but the clock was ticking. His football career was on the line.

Martina's thorough preparation for the journey into the city centre was a little excessive. They arrived in the car park of St James's Hospital at ten past four and had two hours to kill in the outpatients' canteen before the appointment with Dr Singh at six. To make amends for her ultra-punctuality, she talked up a storm: D'Argo's new stores opening in Dublin Airport and on the Stena Seacat; her own busy schedule at work and college. Her retreat from the topic of Luke and his thirty-pound weight gain was blatantly obvious, but something he treated as a blessing in disguise.

'Any news from Ella?' Martina asked as she blew on her steaming cup of coffee.

'I haven't spoken to her in three months,' Luke replied curtly.

Martina stared at him carefully. 'I thought you were keeping in touch with e-mails,' she said.

Luke frowned. 'The only person I e-mail is Ronald,' he said bluntly. This wasn't a sneaky attack at Martina. It was a stone-wall fact. He and Ronald had kept in touch via e-mail ever since he left for Utrecht six months back.

Martina attempted to be diplomatic. 'How is he?' she asked.

'Fine,' Luke replied.

Martina smiled. She was about to needle Luke for an elaboration. He decided to save her the bother.

'He lives in San Francisco now. He took a programming job with Dell and he's engaged to be married,' Luke said bluntly.

Martina was unaware of any of these developments. Luke saw no reason to keep her informed. Considering the speed and heartless manner in which she had broken the poor bloke's heart, her rights to be kept informed of his ongoing personal life were somewhat rescinded. Unwittingly, he had contrived a welcome period of silence. It gave him a chance to glance down at the plaster cast on his right leg. A nervous flush shuddered through his veins. An irrational fear was forming in his head. Once the plaster was cracked open and his repaired leg set free, his wall of excuses would crumble to rubble. He would have to face the world on its own merits and take responsibility for his actions. Nowhere to run to, nowhere to hide.

The grinding whine of the circular saw made Luke gulp

nervously. The chances of suffering an injury from such an instrument were negligible. What made him shrivel with terror was the removal of the plaster cast, his one plausible excuse for his gluttonous downward spiral. Dr Singh stood beside Martina in the cubicle as the nurse gently yanked open the separated plaster with forceps. Luke studied the sickly pale skin he had last laid eyes on in October.

'OK, Luke, on your feet,' Dr Singh said politely.

The pressure applied by such a straightforward request made Luke shiver. He tentatively sat up straight and slowly pressed his cold right heel onto the floor.

'Any discomfort?' Dr Singh said.

Luke looked across at him carefully. Despite his desire to answer yes, he weakly shook his head. Dr Singh bent down on one knee and gently pinched and prodded the shinbone.

'Sit up on the table again, please, Luke,' he said.

Luke co-operated. He glanced across at Martina. She stood there, beaming a proud smile while Dr Singh performed a few more routine tests. It was less than a minute later when the doctor stood up straight and smiled at both mother and son.

'Good as new,' he said happily.

Luke walked from the cubicle with Martina by his side. These first unaided steps since October brought him little satisfaction. He suddenly became aware of his new physique like never before. Up until that moment, it masqueraded amongst the long list of broken leg attachments. The thirty pounds added to his frame were the same as his crutches or the cast, a temporary feature. Both cast and crutches were gone. The flab remained.

'Now, that's that over with,' Martina said positively as the elevator doors shut tight. She and Luke were standing alone inside the steel box. He glanced at her suspiciously.

'What do you mean?' he said.

Martina turned to face him with a smile. 'You know, now that's over with, you can, you know, get back to normal,' she said, faltering badly.

Luke seized upon the expression: ' "Get back to normal" – what do you mean by that?' he said apprehensively. The elevator control panel reported the appliance positioned somewhere between floor three and floor two. Martina had no means of immediate escape. She pushed on bravely with an explanation.

'Well, I mean, now the cast is off you can . . . you know, get out a bit more, get yourself into a new routine—'

'I'm not some freak,' Luke said loudly, interrupting. 'I haven't suddenly become a freak of nature.'

Martina was distraught. She didn't want to make him feel unhappy. 'Luke, I . . .' she said.

It was too late. Luke jabbed a finger at the control panel. The elevator ground to a halt at floor two. As soon as the doors parted he stormed out and hobbled down the corridor towards the staircase. Martina chased after him.

'Luke, where are you going?' she said, blocking his path to the stairs.

'Home,' he replied. 'Alone.'

Martina clapped her mouth shut. She stood face to face with her son, who was obviously in a pit of deep despair. She was on the verge of tears, but knew any further action at this point would only help to make matters worse. Instead, she opened her purse and handed him twenty euros.

'OK,' Martina said softly. 'I'll see you later.'

Luke accepted the money. He frowned at his mother, expelling a tiny portion of the self-loathing that was consuming him from the inside, before moving past her and making his way down the staircase. Outside the hospital, he leaned against a broad granite wall and stared up at the dusky winter sky. He was in a real hole this time. But the worst part was, he could see no way out. The strength, character and determination needed to work his way back to peak physical fitness wasn't inside him. The only tools he had at his disposal were guilt, regret, despair and self-loathing. He took an enormous breath of air before walking towards the hospital exit. Along the way, he caught a glimpse of his bloated frame in a tinted ambulance window. Whether the glass was distorting the facts became irrelevant; another hammer-blow was inflicted on his feeble self-esteem. He came up with a grossly misinformed solution.

McDonald's on Grafton Street was a mile from St James's Hospital. Luke didn't plan on such a long walk for satisfaction, but Thomas Street and Dame Street were short on quick-stop takeaway outlets. This, coupled with his desire for a Big Mac, two large fries, a strawberry milkshake and an ice-cream sundae sealed the deal. It was nearly nine when the binge came to an end. He sat at a table downstairs – alone. The restaurant was deserted. The sense of emptiness he felt inside after such a monstrous intake of calories puzzled him. The food he consumed wasn't filling the hole inside. Somehow, it was being misdirected to other regions of his body, mainly his midriff.

Luke sat staring into space for a good ten minutes before finally deciding to get up and leave. As he climbed the staircase, the first thought to enter his mind was what he could purchase from the vending machines at Pearse Street train station before catching the Dart home. Even now, he was thinking of food. On his way to the exit on the ground floor, he noticed the heavy drops of rain pounding the pavement outside. He stopped short of the door and fiddled with the zip-away hood on the neck of his tracksuit top. He noticed the trio outside almost by accident and pulled back to conceal his presence.

Ten feet down from McDonald's, Peter Swayne, Cecilia and her tiny photographer friend were standing outside the entrance to Lillie's Bordello. The two bouncers on duty stood aside for the photographer and the elegant stride of Cecilia but immediately closed ranks on Swayne. A short conversation and parading of ID did little to persuade them otherwise. They refused to look Swayne in the eye, dismissing his desperate claim in that infuriating manner indicative of bouncers.

Cecilia came back past the bouncers to confer with her 'boyfriend'. Luke expected her photographer friend to join them soon afterwards, but he failed to appear. Luke watched on in fascination. The conversation drifted on. It didn't seem to be going too well for Swayne.

Luke's hunch was spot-on. Cecilia made a concluding statement and shrugged her shoulders before turning and walking in past the bouncers. Swayne was left alone in the pouring rain. He stared past the bouncers in stunned disbelief. Luke couldn't help but giggle. It was a reflex action. However, this giggle soon became another reason for regret. After a painfully long minute standing alone in the deluge, Swayne turned sadly and wandered back up Grafton Street. Only now did Luke dare venture outside McDonald's. He watched his former foe make his way slowly along the deserted thoroughfare, his back hunched against the driving rain.

'Poor bastard,' Luke said quietly.

It didn't seem possible with the poor-me perspective ripe

in his mind, but Luke realised that the old adage, 'There's always someone worse off than yourself,' was accurate and insightful. He waited for Swayne to disappear from view before turning towards Pearse Street train station. His previously strong desire to plunder yet more instant gratification from the vending machines had vanished.

The first two days back on his feet, so to speak, were relatively comfortable for Luke. It was Thursday evening and the return to football that had him sighing anxiously. He packed his kit bag and walked from D'Argo's palace to Killiney train station in silence. A cold, bleak January evening was the setting for his return to football. Woodlawn Park was illuminated by a bevy of amber streetlights posted round the park's perimeter. The other players were already kitted out, performing stretches along the goal line while Jerome paced back and forth across the penalty area like a vigilant general, hands behind his back, inspecting his troops.

'All right, lads?' Luke said, as he walked forward.

The boys nodded their heads or quietly replied, 'All right.' Luke could sense the shock in their faces at the sight of his new appearance. He, Copper, Alan and Edgar were all in the same 5C class, but decked out in his football gear, his armour of glory, the flabby figure before them was a devastating sight to behold.

'You're late,' Jerome said coldly.

Luke turned to face his manager. 'Yeah, sorry,' he replied nervously.

'Right, lads. Three laps, go,' Jerome shouted.

Every player apart from Luke started to jog around the pitch. He threw his kit bag into the centre of the pile behind the goalposts and ran to catch up with his team-mates. The strange sensation of physical exercise had him gasping for breath by the end of the first lap. Muffin and Éclair Burke glanced back sorrowfully as Luke struggled to keep pace with the back markers. They and Edgar decided to cover up the widening gulf by dropping off the pace.

'Lift it, Enders, lift it,' Jerome said deliberately, spotting the subtle helping hand. Luke watched his team-mates sprint clear of him – he was helpless to respond. Midway through lap two he scuttled to a halt by the halfway line and dropped his head to his knees to gather breath.

'Get your head up,' Jerome snapped. 'You won't get air down there.'

Luke watched his manager march away. It was obvious that a grudge had formed in his heart. All through November Jerome had bombarded him with phone calls and personal visits, inviting him to attend the weekend games, offering a makeshift taxi service to and from Killiney. He pestered him endlessly about the diet sheets, urged him to follow the exercise plan. He was the one person who had fought to stem the tide of Luke's collapse into oblivion. But for every attempt he made to help, Luke would find an excuse – some reason to dodge the reality. It was heartbreaking to watch someone with a second chance at the dream throw it all away. But there was only so much energy a man with a business and a football team to run could expend on one player who continually shunned his attempts at aid.

'Luke,' Jerome yelled.

The Enders had formed a neat circle round their manager near the goalpost after completing the third lap. Luke jogged slowly across to join up with them.

'Right, get into groups of three and spread out, five yards apart,' Jerome said.

It was the ultimate nightmare for Luke. Circuit training, which meant separate stations for short sprinting, push-ups, sit-ups, squats, star jumps. The sharp squeal of Jerome's silver whistle signalled the start and end of each three-minute circuit. In every single section of the training session Luke collapsed in exhaustion before completing the task at hand. He was a shadow of his former self. It was discouraging for the other players to watch their captain embarrass himself time and time again. The effect of losing such an influential figure had already cost them dearly.

The Stretford Enders had lost five league games between October and January and slipped to third place in Division B. They also surrendered their All-Ireland Cup crown, defeated five–one at home by Rathdale Athletic of all teams. The one bright spot in the darkness was the growing speculation involving Ille's future. It seemed Man Utd, Liverpool and Arsenal were all waiting to offer him a trial that summer. This news should have brought a smile to Luke's face, but jealousy intervened. Another one moving on, making the grade, while he floundered deep in the quicksand.

'Right, boys, good work tonight. We'll finish up with a seven-a-side,' Jerome announced.

Luke puffed a sigh of relief. Football – he could still play football. This was the perfect opportunity to utilise his natural skill and experience on the pitch to cover up his abysmal loss of physical fitness.

'Two-touch,' Jerome shouted.

The game kicked off. Luke decided to stay central, spraying the ball left and right to his super-fit team-mates, who could make all the runs forward.

Unfortunately, it didn't work out that way.

There was no chance to settle on the ball. The tackles

came flying in too quickly. Luke was a liability. Unable to defend, unable to motivate the attack, he gave away countless free-kicks by taking more than the mandatory two touches. Soon his team-mates were tutting and sighing in frustration.

This was the final straw.

Ille was running the show for the opposition. His quicksilver footwork, lightning-fast runs off the ball and clever one-touch passing dictated the pattern of play. Eventually Luke lost his cool at the sight of such a skilful performance. He lashed out in a horrid fashion.

Ille knocked a ball through his legs and manoeuvred past him. That is, until Luke swung his newly healed right shinbone across Ille's left kneecap. The little Romanian wizard crashed to the ground, screaming in agony. The other players gathered round, checking on the injury sustained by their chief playmaker. Jerome stopped the play and ran over to check on Ille's left knee before helping him to his feet.

Luke was left to his own devices, crumpled in a flabby, sweaty heap. After making sure no serious damage was done, Jerome reared on his former captain like a cornered rat.

'What's your problem?' he shouted.

'What?' Luke replied.

This was the most shattering blow yet. His team-mates stood together as one, staring at him over the shoulder of their manager, the ringleader of the hatred and bile pointing in one clear-cut direction. Luke was on the verge of tears but tried to fight his corner.

'It was an accident,' he pleaded.

No one replied. Ille looked across at him, still smarting from the terrible tackle that could easily have ended up with him taking a ride in the back of an ambulance. It was obvious which way public opinion had shifted. Luke had become the Enders' enemy number one. He decided to save them the bother of having to act on their convictions.

'Fine, I'm going,' he announced.

Jerome and the Enders watched their fallen idol pack his things together and walk from Woodlawn Park alone. Memories were short in Dun Laoghaire. His journey from saviour and cult hero to villain of the piece was sickeningly swift. It was a cruel way to treat a friend.

How the Mighty Have Fallen

Luke had to wait twenty-five minutes at Dun Laoghaire train station for a Dart to bring him home, thanks to an accident involving an articulated lorry and a bread van at a level crossing near Sydney Parade. It gave him valuable thinking time. Football had always been his one true love, or so he had believed. But the sheer speed with which something he dedicated his life to had betrayed this devotion stung badly.

By the time the Dart arrived, the thought occurred to him, Why do I want to be a footballer? Who am I doing it for? The answers to such simple questions proved strangely elusive. Perhaps this dream he clung to so dearly was a superbly crafted fiction and something that would ultimately leave him feeling hollow inside. David Swayne crossed his mind. Football was everything to him, but in the end it wasn't enough. He didn't come to the drastic decision to end his own life because Everton turned him away. There was more to it than that. Life wasn't worth living in David's eyes for reasons other than football. He could have made it as a professional, if it meant so much to him. The problem or problems that had persuaded him to end it all had nothing to do with football.

Luke opened the front door of D'Argo's palace and keyed in the security code to disable the alarm system. There was no one home to greet him, for a change. He turned on the hall and living-room lights and closed the door behind him. It was all a matter of willpower. He kept his sight trained on the floor in front of him and marched straight towards his bedroom. Once inside, he undressed and stepped into the en suite shower. He kept his eyes shut. He found it hard enough to scrub his flabby gut, let alone stare at it in all its naked splendour. After his wash, Luke wrapped a large white beach towel around his waist and sat down at his computer desk. He peered down at the bottom drawer and tentatively pulled it open.

He lifted out the contract and stared at the club crest on the front page. Michael Turner had been e-mailing him since October asking for updates on his progress. Luke replied diligently to each electronic enquiry – obviously forgetting to mention his ballooning weight and deepening depression. But now, in the aftermath of his training disaster, he realised the contract wasn't worth the paper it was written on. Football did not stand still. Michael Turner's claim that Luke was the most promising talent he had witnessed in twenty years could be old news by now. The reality was simple. If he couldn't shed the excess weight and return to fitness in the space of ten weeks, he would miss the professional football boat, permanently.

To celebrate this stark realisation, Luke made a bee-line for the kitchen and loaded up on sugar, salt and fat. Turning over a new leaf wasn't the kind of task undertaken on an empty stomach. Anyway, what difference would another two pounds make?

The next evening, Luke gasped and sighed his way up Killiney hill after school. In the fading winter daylight he noticed the outline of a sleek Ford Probe parked at the end of the long winding driveway that led to D'Argo's palace. It brought a bitter tut from his throat. He was in no mood to sit through a heartfelt apology.

Luke closed the front door behind him. Immediately he noticed the conversation between Jerome and Martina in the living room come to an abrupt halt. He regretted his noisy entrance, realising a more subtle approach would have afforded him the opportunity to earwig the discussion, which he was certain revolved around his shocking weight gain.

'Luke,' Martina said as he walked directly towards his bedroom. He stopped and turned towards her and Jerome, who appeared from the living room.

'Can we talk?' Jerome said quickly.

Luke sighed. This wasn't a question he could answer freely. He marched past them into the living room and took a seat on one of the expensive brown leather armchairs. Martina and Jerome sat on the couch, forming an informal inter-rogation committee.

'Luke, I've come here to say sorry,' Jerome said softly. He paused for a breath. Luke eyeballed him fiercely.

'I realise I've let you down. I should have helped you through this injury. It's just . . .'

This time the pause was for careful consideration. How to phrase the words 'fat blob' in a tactful manner. Martina realised she was a third wheel. She stood up to leave.

'I'll make some more tea,' she said.

Jerome felt her caressing hand on his shoulder briefly. It was obvious a heart-to-heart pep talk was on the cards. Luke suddenly felt nauseous. The man who had cruelly hurled abuse his way and discarded him from his precious football team less than twenty-four hours earlier bowed his head in a sorrowful manner.

'I've let you down, Luke. The same way I let David down,' he said sadly.

Luke paid close attention. This was sure to be good.

'I keep thinking about the final in June,' Jerome said. He raised his head. 'That was seven months ago. How could I let all this happen in seven months?' Jerome had a tear running down his cheek.

'I should have done something, Luke. I should have talked him round, made him see sense.' Jerome broke down into a pitiful sob. 'How could I just abandon him?' he pleaded.

It was a sincere question. Jerome Barnes was heartbroken by the death of David Swayne – he always would be. It was clear he blamed himself for letting David drift away from his precious football team. This was an exercise in arrogance. Who said it had anything to do with football? Why did everyone just assume this to be the reason? Anyway, Luke knew who was *really* to blame. He was the one who had stood face-to-face with the troubled soul on the side of Dalkey quarry, some five hundred yards from the living room they were sitting in that very minute. If anyone could have talked him round, it was Luke.

Jerome wiped the tears from his eyes. He stared at Luke with a potent mix of passion and determination. 'It's not gonna happen again, Luke. I'll make amends. We'll start tomorrow morning, me and you. I guarantee I'll have you back to normal by the end of March.'

It was these three little words, 'back to normal'. They were the spark that lit the fuse.

'You'd like that, wouldn't you? Help train the fat kid back to fitness. That would give your ego a real shot in the arm,' Luke said angrily.

Jerome tried to reply.

'Save it for someone who cares. I'm not your little science project,' Luke said bitterly. 'I broke my leg giving everything for your stupid football team. And what thanks do I get? None. But now you've decided to soothe your conscience, all of a sudden you want to help me. No way.'

Luke stormed out of the living room. Martina blocked his path down the hall. He turned to face Jerome.

'It's not like that, Luke. You know me well enough by now,' Jerome said quietly. This was true. He wasn't a man built on the principle of 'all show, no substance'. He would never pledge to do something unless he planned to see it through to the end. His work ethic was impeccable. But Luke needed to salvage his pride.

'I don't want to be trained. I don't want to be a footballer. I just want to be left alone,' he explained.

Luke slung his schoolbag next to the coat hanger in the hallway and walked out the front door. Martina and Jerome stood side by side and watched him go. It was a sad moment, but offering to help someone who does not want to be helped is a complete waste of time.

Jerome fished his coat from the hanger. He looked at Martina. 'If he changes his mind, ring me,' he said.

Martina nodded sadly. Jerome didn't wave goodbye before walking to his car. On his way down Vico Road he passed Luke, who was wandering towards Killiney train station. For a moment he considered stopping, but all the talking had been done. It was up to Luke now.

What was originally a trip outside to escape the stifling attention of his mother and Jerome soon became an opportunity to binge. Luke headed to Dun Laoghaire and exchanged two euros at the Burke Family Bakery for a bag of jam doughnuts. He needed a low-key location to consume his stash in the slobbish manner he had adopted over the past three months. As darkness descended on the harbour he walked along the north pier. He wanted to get as far away from civilisation as possible. This meant a trip to the automated lighthouse, which guaranteed privacy in the chilly winter evenings. The gentle slosh of the water against the base of the harbour wall formed a soothing soundtrack.

Luke opened the bag and devoured the first doughnut with four clean chomps. What enjoyment he derived from such speedy swallows was questionable. All that mattered was the continuous food-chewing motion. The sight of the Seacat moored across at the south pier brought back memories of the summer. The numerous journeys to and from Holyhead – six separate voyages. David made but two. Luke felt guilt creep up his spine again. He repelled the sensation with a sugar-coated doughnut injection. The sound of footsteps nearby became apparent in the peaceful atmosphere. He turned his head to investigate. It took a long, careful stare to identify the tall, broad figure that came to a halt twenty feet away at the edge of the pier.

'What are you doing here?' Swayne said.

Luke stood up straight to answer him, but before he could reply a nasty smile was forming on the face of his arch-nemesis.

'Is that your fourth or fifth bag?' he said with a snigger.

Luke frowned. He stuffed the Burke Family Bakery bag inside his jacket pocket and prepared a counter-attack. He wanted it to seem relevant and natural as a retort. But he couldn't resist going straight for the jugular, no matter how abstract it might seem.

'Still getting refused from Lillie's?' Luke said.

The smile soon slid off Swayne's face. He was stunned by Luke's intimate knowledge of something he considered a purely private affair.

'You must keep asking yourself, "What's camera-boy got

that I haven't?" ' Luke said spitefully. It was a knockout blow, but by no means a fair punch. Luke noticed the complete shutdown in Swayne. He wasn't incensed to the point of physical violence. He didn't snarl or shout something detrimental about Honchee northsiders. He simply imploded, stuffing both hands inside his jacket pockets and slumping onto a nearby granite bench.

Luke felt awful. There was no pleasure in seeing Swayne unhappy. He stared across at his wounded opponent for almost a minute before joining him on the bench.

'Sorry,' Luke muttered.

Swayne glanced sideways. 'What for? You're right,' he replied sadly.

It was something Luke never dreamed possible. Himself and Swayne sitting down together and talking. It wasn't an awkward situation. On the contrary, the company of another person was a relief.

'I can't believe she went in without you,' Luke said.

'Yeah,' Swayne replied, eventually.

Silently Luke said, 'I can't believe she came on to Tonka at your brother's funeral.' The Lillie's incident was bad enough; what happened in the courtyard outside the Melting Pot would really bring him to his knees.

'Are you still together?' Luke asked.

Swayne stared at his feet. 'No,' he replied.

Luke spoke silently again. 'You're better off without her,' he said. Swayne cocked his head at that precise moment and looked at Luke as if he could read his mind.

Luke gulped. 'What?' he said.

Swayne kept staring: he seemed to be on the verge of a smile. 'I've got something to give you,' he said.

Luke and Swayne caught the 46A to Baker's Corner together,

then walked to Merrion Park estate. They didn't exchange more than ten words on the journey but somehow spending time in each other's company wasn't an uncomfortable experience. It was only when they approached Merrion Grove that Luke started to shuffle hesitantly.

'What's wrong?' Swayne said, turning to Luke, who halted on the pavement outside his front garden.

Luke stared at the front door and gulped. The last time he had called into the Swayne household, David was out in the garden shed, preparing to hang himself. It sent a cold shiver down his spine.

'Are you OK?' Swayne enquired flatly.

Luke snapped out of it. He focused on Swayne and nodded. The walk to the porch door felt like the approach to a haunted house on a hilltop. The fumble of keys reverberated like a thousand plate-glass windows shattered by a huge explosion. The rasping screech of the porch door, screaming for oil as it lurched open, frayed his nerves still further. His heartbeat accelerated out of control. He was a murderer, returning to the scene of his crime.

'Ma,' Swayne said loudly, upon stepping through the front door.

Luke stepped inside the porch, but ventured no further. He watched Swayne walk to the kitchen door and push it open. His mother sat at the kitchen table beyond, staring blankly into space. She didn't bother to acknowledge him. He retreated sadly, shutting the door behind him. Luke trembled inside as Swayne approached. Any moment now he would unearth the dark secret. He would recognise the guilt written in dark, bold capital letters across his face and would claim revenge on his brother's murderer.

'This way,' Swayne said, turning off towards the staircase.

Luke puffed a sigh of relief. He considered baling out,

then and there. But with a few seconds to compose himself he found the strength to carry on. He followed Swayne up the staircase into the unknown. Each step along the way had a familiar ring to it, but at the top, where he and Tonka would normally turn left and enter the box room, Luke stepped into the back bedroom. The one place he had never thought to venture.

Swayne's bedroom was an enthralling sight. Man Utd posters covered the walls. A long single bed was squashed beneath the windowsill beside a broad, black wardrobe. The remainder of the room consisted of body-building equipment. A bench press, various silver bars, a collection of screw-on weights and a selection of dumbbells.

'Have a seat,' Swayne said. He was positioned on the bench press, leaving Luke to squat on the corner of his bed. They stared at one another, not quite sure what should happen next.

'Where is it?' Luke said.

'What?' Swayne replied in surprise.

'This thing – this thing you wanted to give me,' Luke explained.

Swayne's momentary lapse of concentration had passed. He nodded his head and left the room. 'I'll be back in a second,' he said.

Swayne closed the door behind him and shuffled down the staircase. Luke had no choice but to nose about the place. It was the only reasonable way to pass the time. The first thing to catch his attention was the wooden bulletin board on the wall beside the wardrobe. It was stuffed full of photographs. He moved in for a closer inspection. Cecilia, Cecilia and Swayne, Cecilia and her friends, Cecilia and her first-year pupil of the year award. There had to be fifty separate snaps. Not to mention a host of magazine cuttings of the little minx in action. Pride of place belonged to a faded Polaroid in the centre of the board. It was Cecilia and Swayne together, entwined as one. They stared at one another, both smiling, with undoubted expressions of love.

The heavy thud of footsteps grew louder. Swayne was climbing the staircase. Luke pretended to examine the dumbbells with great regard.

'Here,' Swayne said, upon opening the bedroom door.

He handed Luke a TDK cassette tape: written on the label of side A was 'Mix Tape 3'. It took Luke a moment to recall the memory. Terry Culshaw's house, after the first trial. Luke, Tonka and David preparing for the Wednesday night disco in the Vortex with Stacy. David performing a rendition of 'Tracks of My Tears'. When they returned home to Dublin, David had borrowed the tape from Luke. He had forgotten to return it.

'Thanks,' Luke said quietly.

Swayne moved across the room and picked up the largest set of dumbbells. Luke watched him pump the heavy weights with consummate ease. He pretended to fake an interest in body-building. But his real craving was to siphon some info on Cecilia and camera-boy.

'Who is camera-boy, anyway?' he asked bluntly.

Swayne hesitated briefly before answering, 'His name's Giovanni. He works for her agency.'

Swayne continued to pump iron. It seemed to provide him with catharsis. Luke was still desperate for more details. He selected his next question carefully. In retrospect, it was far from tactful.

'So, who dumped who?' he demanded.

Swayne finished his set of exercises before laying the dumbbells back on the floor. He took several deep breaths before turning to face Luke. He opened his mouth to answer but paused without a syllable. Some kind of internal debate raged on inside his mind. The result was a victory for candour.

'She dumped me,' Swayne said sadly. 'She always dumps me.'

It summed up what Luke had always suspected in a single sentence. Cecilia resorted to Swayne the same way a trapeze artist resorts to a safety net – when all else fails. He was starting to consider his one-time tormentor in a completely different light. He even offered words of comfort.

'You're better off without her,' Luke said bluntly. 'In my opinion.'

Swayne leaned back against a long silver bar mounted on the bench press. He stared into space thoughtfully, then turned to Luke and confessed.

'I can't help it. I love her, I've always loved her. Ever since we were eight years old. The first day of third year in Woodlawn Primary with Mrs Foran, I fell in love with Cecilia Giles.'

The full picture finally came into focus. The persistent harassment Luke had suffered at the hands of Swayne when he first arrived in Dun Laoghaire two years back had more to do with an instinct to defend his territorial claim over Cecilia than an out-and-out hatred of all things northside.

'What about you and Ella?' Swayne said, derailing Luke's train of thought.

Luke faced Swayne, who patiently awaited an answer. The same internal battle played out in his mind. This was a mortal enemy probing him for sensitive information. Was it wise to divulge sincerely or renege on the trust displayed and answer with fractious caution. Suddenly, it occurred to him, he had nothing to gain by playing his cards close to his chest.

'We split up,' he said.

Swayne nodded his head. 'Why?' he replied.

Luke watched him begin another circuit of dumbbell exercises. It was the first time anyone had asked him to explain. Ella hadn't bothered ringing to find out why he dropped the bombshell before she boarded her flight to London. Martina's questions were consistently spurned. And yet, somehow, Swayne deserved an answer.

'She's in London and I'm stuck here. It just wouldn't work, long distance. At least now we can both move on with things.'

Luke's explanation was perfectly reasonable. He did feel better saying the actual words. He no longer felt guilty about ending it with Ella because of his own selfish reasons and insecurities. Swayne seemed to accept the statement as fact. But he had a second question.

'What happened to you?' he said.

Luke knew exactly what he was talking about, but pleaded ignorance. 'What do you mean?' he asked coyly.

Swayne didn't bother explaining. He simply stared at Luke. Eventually, he conceded the point.

'I eat like a pig from morning to night, seven days a week. That's what happened to me. I'm a flabby fuck,' Luke said sadly.

Swayne didn't take advantage. He wore a neutral expression, but one clearly leaning towards sympathetic. Luke looked at his enemy, quietly pumping iron. This was a golden opportunity to open his heart.

'I have a two-year professional contract at home. If I pass a medical in April I'll sign a deal with Preston North End,' Luke explained. He glanced at a full-length mirror pinned to the back of Swayne's bedroom door. His reflection said it all. 'But I won't pass that medical.'

Swayne stopped pumping iron. 'Why not?' he said.

Luke couldn't bring himself to look Swayne in the eye. 'Because I can't be bothered any more,' he replied. 'I don't know how to fight back.'

Swayne didn't understand. Luke would have to elaborate further.

'Every time I got knocked down I'd stand up ready for more. You know that more than anyone,' he said. It took a while to force the words from his lips and admit the horrible truth publicly. 'But now, I keep asking myself, What's the point? Who cares about playing football? Who cares about anything?'

Swayne finished his set of exercises. He stood up from the bench press and patted his sweat-laden temple with a small white towel. Luke watched his movements like a preying cheetah studying a grazing gazelle from the cover of the long grass. Somehow, he sensed deep insight hidden within the impressive chest of Peter Swayne.

'Can I ask you one question?' he said.

Luke nodded. Swayne looked him straight in the eye.

'Do *you* want to play football?' he said.

At first, Luke shrugged his shoulders. It was a blunt, but refreshingly direct approach from Swayne. The moral and intellectual debate raging through Luke's mind over the past twenty-four hours had eluded the one true issue. The only question worth asking. Did he want to do it?

'Yeah,' Luke said.

Swayne sat back down on the bench press. 'I can help you. If you help me,' he said.

Luke was bemused by the request. It seemed an obtuse and vague suggestion.

'You need a trainer. Someone to work out an exercise programme and a sensible diet. But more than that, you need someone to make you stick to it,' Swayne explained.

'You're gonna do that?' Luke replied doubtfully.

Swayne nodded his head. 'For a price,' he said.

Luke sunk deeper into the well of quandary. What could Swayne possibly want from him?

'Which is?' Luke prompted.

Swayne seemed reluctant to finalise the small print of the deal. Luke's mind ran with some pretty wild speculation for the thirty seconds or so of silence that intervened. Eventually, he blurted it out.

'Well, I'll train you . . .' Swayne stuttered. 'If you help me win Cecilia back.'

Luke didn't laugh, smirk, grin, or snigger. He couldn't bring himself to articulate his feelings. It was such a bolt from the blue. Irony had no jurisdiction in this scenario. This was a galaxy far, far away from irony.

Swayne grew impatient. 'Well?' he said.

Luke was still paralysed by the request.

'Look, it's very simple. I help you, you help me,' Swayne said impatiently. This was more like it. The old Peter Swayne he knew and loathed. What might have been construed as an act of kindness to a lonely soul was in fact a calculated snare to set up a business deal. The world was a bizarre place, but not so far gone that Luke Farrell and Peter Swayne could become friends.

'So, is it a deal?' Swayne said.

Luke peered down at the outstretched hand. It seemed absurd, but once more it came down to his current situation. He had little to lose. 'Deal,' he said firmly.

FIRST THINGS FIRST

Luke stood outside room nine in the Foster Caine mall, awaiting the arrival of Miss Court for 5C's French class. He stared blankly across at the hectic hustle and bustle of pupils and teachers moving in and out of classrooms. There were no clear images, just a jumble of shapes. Then something to his far right caught Luke's attention. He focused in. A group of second years, led by a tall blond streak of piss, had separated and surrounded one of their classmates inside the alcove adjacent to the career guidance counsellor's office. He was small, round, with chubby red cherub cheeks and a tragic pudding bowl haircut.

Blondie discreetly issued a warning. Chubby then handed over a sum of money. He received a patronising pat on the cheek before Blondie and his crew dispersed. They sauntered past Luke and made their exit from the Foster Caine mall. Luke turned to Chubby, who picked up his schoolbag sadly and trundled past. For a moment, Luke reached out his hand to stop him. He could offer protection and words of comfort. But he withdrew his hand just as quickly. He was in no condition to champion the cause of others.

'Farrell,' a voice called firmly.

Luke turned to Swayne, who stood at the entrance to the mall. He walked past several members of Co waiting for the French class to reach Luke. Neither Swayne nor Co uttered a single word of greeting to one another. Ever since Niall

Casey – Swayne's right-hand man – debunked to the Institute of Education on Leason Street to acquire a stellar Leaving Cert, Co – Peter Swayne's one-time gang of under-lings and lackeys – had fallen apart and disbanded. It left a chief without Indians, a general without an army, Swayne without friends.

'Have you got a weighing scales at home?' he said openly.

Luke cringed. He gestured with the palm of his hand for a volume reduction and spun his neck left and right to check the reaction of his classmates.

'Yeah, why?' he replied eventually.

'Meet me at the bike shed, quarter to four,' Swayne ordered. He retreated from the mall with the minimum of fuss, leaving Luke to wonder what fate awaited him. Before serious internal debate could begin, Mrs Court arrived and ushered her students inside room nine.

Swayne stared in mild disbelief at the exterior of D'Argo's palace. The majestic perimeter wall, the detailed landscaped garden, the nine-foot-high security gates. It was too good to be true.

'You fell on your feet this time, Honchee,' Swayne said with a smile.

Luke turned sharply. 'What will I call you?' he said. 'Swayne?'

It was an excellent point. Circumstances had forced them together. The old articles of war were obsolete. It was time for a first-name basis.

'My name is Luke,' Luke insisted. He stared at Swayne, awaiting a response. He didn't say anything, merely nodded his head in agreement. That would do fine. They continued inside the house. The surprise of the day came with the sound of Martina's voice.

'Hi,' she said brightly. Luke and Swayne halted in the hallway like two bungling cat-burglars caught in the act. Martina had company. Jude, her personal assistant, was enjoying a cup of tea at the kitchen counter.

Luke glanced at Swayne, whom he would have to introduce to Martina. 'Erm, Ma, this is Peter Swayne,' he mumbled anxiously.

'Oh,' she replied unintentionally. The reasons for surprise were twofold. Firstly, the issue of David's death was still fresh in people's minds and affected their behaviour in his presence. Their awkward attempts to sidestep reality created a superficial vacuum of pity. It made Swayne's life a living hell. Secondly, this was the infamous 'Swayne', the evil bully who had made Luke's life a misery when he arrived in Dun Laoghaire two years back. The best cover-up tactic Martina could manage was a timid handshake and a nonsensical introduction.

'This is Jude, Peter. My personal assistant,' she bumbled. Jude handled the bizarre segue with an effortless smile and wave of her hand. Luke intervened quickly to save everyone from his mother.

'This way,' he said to Swayne. They made their way down the hall to Luke's bedroom. Now the real work could begin.

'OK, stand up,' Swayne said.

Luke looked at him doubtfully. He had taken off his runners to help fight the tide, but what awaited him when he stepped off the varnished wood floor onto the Boots Easiscale would not be pretty.

Swayne glanced at his watch. 'Today, if possible,' he remarked coldly.

Luke sighed. He mournfully stepped onto the scales. The

number dial spun forward at a furious pace. When it shuddered to a halt the grim news read . . .

'Seventy-seven kilos. Twelve stone three,' Swayne said bluntly. Luke peered down at the numbers in disbelief. In the space of three months he had gone from a trim ten stone to a tank-like twelve. It didn't seem possible.

'All right, hop off,' Swayne said. After a moment of morbid self-loathing Luke obeyed the order. It was a while before he could find the strength to lift his sunken head. When he did, he saw Swayne jotting down figures in a small green notepad. It was purely academic to him, just a number on a page. For Luke, it represented the end.

'Right – stand up against your bedroom door. Shoulders straight, head forward,' Swayne said. Luke slunk across his bedroom floor like a condemned criminal being measured for his coffin. Swayne produced a tape measure from his jacket pocket and unfurled a length of sheet metal, starting from top to bottom.

'Hold this steady,' he said to Luke, handing him the start of the measuring tape level with his crown. Swayne slid the measuring tape down to the ground, double-checking the final number twice before confirming the result verbally.

'One hundred and seventy-four centimetres,' he said.

Luke wasn't quite up with the metric system. 'What's that?' he demanded.

Swayne jotted the number down in his notebook before replying. 'Five foot nine,' he said.

Luke nodded. Swayne put the tape measure back inside his pocket and pulled out a small white book. It was a glossy job, with a healthy family on the front cover, all sporting tracksuits, perfect pearly whites and unfeasibly cheerful smiles.

'OK. Take your top off,' Swayne said. The request came right out of the blue.

Luke was suitably astonished. 'What?' he replied.

'Take your top off,' Swayne said slowly. He seemed to think Luke was hard of hearing. But the problem wasn't audio related.

'Why?' Luke said. Swayne didn't understand what all the fuss was about. Then again, he had a midriff sculpted like a slab of granite and pecs and biceps crying out for a dousing in Johnson's Baby Oil. This was a definite impasse. Luke would no longer blindly follow orders. He wanted explanations.

'Look, don't get excited. I just want to see what shape you're in,' Swayne explained.

'Why?' Luke fired back like a bullet.

Swayne sighed. He took a deep, deep breath. 'If I'm going to train you, I need to know what kind of shape you're in physically, and therefore understand what kind of exercise you can manage.'

Fair point. No arguing with such logic. Luke moaned quietly under his breath before lifting his T-shirt over his head. His naked body felt exposed, especially under the spotlight of male eyes. Swayne didn't flinch, he examined each contour carefully, lifting up Luke's arms, prodding and pinching like a doctor.

'Right, put your top back on,' he said finally.

While Luke dressed, Swayne sat down at the computer table and muttered to himself while studying the figures in his little green notebook. Luke sat on the corner of his bed, patiently awaiting the verdict of his personal trainer. Swayne bobbed his head about in the style necessary to conduct of mental arithmetic. He finally looked up at him.

'Two stone in eight weeks. No problem,' he announced confidently.

Luke actually smiled.

'You're still in good condition, physically. All we need to do is reduce your calorie intake and implement a fitness regime to regain your stamina,' Swayne said.

The sound of the front door shutting resounded clearly. Swayne and Luke stopped and listened to approaching footsteps. A few moments later there was a knock on the bedroom door.

'Luke,' Martina said.

'Come on in,' he replied. She opened the bedroom door slowly. Jude had obviously left the house moments earlier. Swayne pounced on this opportunity. He stood up politely.

'Miss Farrell,' he said. Martina acknowledged his mannerly address with her undivided attention. 'Could I ask a favour?' he added politely. Luke was intrigued, Martina likewise. They waited on his next sentence with bated breath.

Luke stood on the verge of the kitchen, watching with a ghostly expression of bemusement. Swayne regurgitated the same clichéd phrases time and time again – 'No pain, no gain', 'If it's not there, you can't eat it', 'Don't start tomorrow what you can start today', and hummed in agreement with Martina's views on the power of personal motivation. Together they loaded a brown cardboard box that had originally contained one-kilo bags of oatmeal with precious junk food. Biscuits, chocolate bars, crisps, sweets, anything with the power to draw a gratifying 'Mmm' was removed from the fridge and cupboards.

'Peanuts have protein,' Luke pleaded desperately.

Swayne tossed a large bag of KP dry roasted into the box. 'They're also sky-high in fat,' he replied.

Luke stood by and watched, helpless to intervene. Martina was warming to Peter Swayne. They continued their discussion on health and exercise as the kitchen was drained dry of foil-wrapped reality escape routes. Before long, a second cardboard box was called for. It included a stack of tins. Rice pudding, custard, cream, a tub of pistachio Häagen Dazs and a packet of red liquorice.

Swayne and Martina stood back from the empty cupboards, surveying their purge with a sense of pride. Luke wandered in to inspect the massacre. He felt a new strain of loneliness infect his bloodstream. Reality had hammered a wrecking ball against his flimsy house of cards.

'Thanks for your help, Miss Farrell,' Swayne said.

'No, thank you, Peter,' Martina replied. The newly formed alliance took a well-earned three-minute break before collecting the two cardboard boxes from the kitchen counter and walking to the open front door. Luke trailed behind them like a pursuing TV news cameraman and saw the booty placed on the front seat of D'Argo's silver Cherokee Jeep. She walked round to the driver's door.

'Luke, I'll be home early tonight,' she said. He muttered the word 'traitor' under his breath. Swayne stood on the driveway and watched Martina start the engine. He smiled and waved goodbye as the Jeep manoeuvred down the driveway, stopping at the security gates. Only now did he turn to face Luke.

'Right, let's go shopping,' Swayne said.

An hour later, Luke and Swayne were wandering round the spacious aisles of Tesco in the Bloomfield shopping centre, filling a trolley with fruit, vegetables and a host of healthy, nutritious snack treats. The incentive of a fifty per cent discount available at any D'Argo store wasn't enough to entice Luke through the door. He insisted they go elsewhere. 'Stupid low-fat yoghurts,' he muttered bitterly, as he continued to bemoan his fortune.

'Jesus, could you shut up moaning for five minutes, please?' Swayne said. He picked out a ripe bunch of bananas and placed them on the weighing scales. It was the first time he had snapped at Luke's perpetual complaining. After an hour of 'Poor me this, poor me that', Swayne had had enough.

He turned and faced Luke. 'Look, you're in a hole. Right?'

Luke was determined to sulk, but eventually nodded his head.

'So, this is the way out of the hole,' Swayne concluded.

Luke peered at the contents of the trolley. Apples, oranges, pears, peaches, bananas, kiwis, a wide range of fruit choices. Spanish onions, tomatoes, cucumbers, iceberg lettuce, potatoes. Cans of tuna, skinless chicken fillets, low-fat milk and yoghurt. Bottles of mineral water, diet Coke and Lucozade Sport. There wasn't one item that could be construed as sinful.

'One more thing,' Swayne said. He directed the trolley to the crisp aisle. Luke's eyes brightened at the sight of salty indulgence. Swayne reached onto a shelf and retrieved a six-pack of plain popcorn.

'If you need to snack, this is your best bet. High in fibre, carbohydrates, reasonably low in fat,' he said.

Luke smiled.

'However, stick with plain popcorn. Not buttered, not toffee and not cheese flavoured,' he added.

Luke frowned.

When they returned to D'Argo's palace, the first job was to restock the barren cupboards with their healthy swag. It was a job conducted in near silence – that is, until Swayne started asking questions. Questions that were completely unrelated to health and fitness.

'Remember when you came to Dun Laoghaire?' he asked.

Luke was busy arranging the fruit bowl. 'What about it?' he replied.

Swayne took a moment to phrase his next question properly. 'Why was Cecilia mad about you?' he asked quietly.

Luke stopped arranging fruit. It was an interesting question for Swayne to be asking. After all, he should understand the unique idiosyncrasies that formed Cecilia Giles better than anyone else.

They faced one another.

Luke dropped his eyes to the floor. Apparently Swayne was unaware of the driving force behind his sometime girl-friend. This conversation was drifting towards the arena of touchy subject.

'What is it?' Swayne demanded softly.

Luke looked him in the eye. It was time to test the old adage, Honesty is the best policy.

'Well,' he started reluctantly, 'Cecilia is a . . .'

Swayne was left out to dry by his untimely pause. This was a tricky situation. Luke wanted to mutter 'Forget it' and scurry off to his room with a big bag of bacon fries.

'Is a what?' Swayne said persistently.

Luke had no choice but to finish what he had started. '. . . is a glamour junkie,' he said.

There was no instant reaction of violence. Swayne seemed more confused than upset. Luke decided to elaborate on his statement before his burly ex-enemy came to a disagreeable conclusion.

'See, when I arrived on the scene I was an unknown quantity. She finds that exciting. Like this photographer dude, he's just the latest craze. Once that initial buzz of excitement passes and he's no longer a mystery she'll get bored and move on.'

Swayne turned to face Luke. For a second the future looked bleak as the expression on his face began to change. But a snarl never materialised. Instead, a forlorn look surfaced on an already downhearted disposition.

'You're right,' Swayne said sadly. 'That's her down to a T.' He walked away from Luke and sat down at the kitchen counter, lowering his head in a sorrowful bow.

Luke put aside his own catalogue of misfortunes and felt a pang of guilt. His accurate description of Cecilia brought home the sense of loss to Swayne. It was his duty to resurrect hope.

'But listen, that doesn't mean you're out of the running,' he said brightly. Swayne lifted his head up a notch. 'All we have to do is work out a way to re-ignite her passion.'

Luke spoke the words and implied an upbeat, optimistic sentiment. However, all he could hear in his mind was, 'He hasn't a hope in hell.' Cecilia had moved on from her 'cute boys in my class' phase. Her sights were now set on much loftier targets. Footballers, up and coming pop stars and actors, wealthy whizz-kid millionaires. Money, power, talent or a bright future. Swayne had none of these qualities. The time allotted for silent contemplation expired. Swayne seemed to derive some sense of hope from Luke's words. He stood up from the kitchen counter, manufactured a brave smile and went back to unpacking the shopping bags.

Luke remained frozen to the spot. A flash of inspiration, a brainwave to end all brainwaves, had wormed its way inside his head. He studied Swayne carefully and began to smile. The perfect plan to hold up his end of the bargain was coming together nicely.

* * *

It had been a long day. Between trips to Dun Laoghaire, casual conversations concerning Cecilia Giles and the whole-sale revolution of his eating habits, Luke was ready for bed at half nine. However, before he could return home from Swayne's house, one more task needed to be completed. Swayne led the way to his bedroom. Luke followed close behind.

'Right, this is your schedule,' he said quietly.

Luke was handed a set of stapled A4 pages. It was a seven-day menu, Monday to Sunday. The headings of BREAKFAST, LUNCH, DINNER and SNACKS were laid out in dark, bold capital letters. Beneath which was the set meal. It was an accurate account. Exact measurements, grams, ounces, millilitres, the works. Luke had enough trouble understanding the abbreviations for table- and teaspoons.

'I'll be eating with you for the first week. I'll show you how to prepare some of the dinners,' Swayne said.

Luke nodded. 'What about the training routine?' he said. When he looked up from the sheets he noticed Swayne changing out of his T-shirt. It was obvious he made good use of the exercise equipment that dominated the landscape of his bedroom. His chest and shoulders were enormous, but his waist and stomach were trim and lean.

'We start tomorrow morning, seven a.m.,' Swayne said. 'I'll call for you.'

'What will we be doing?' Luke asked anxiously. After the debacle of the Enders' training session he was somewhat edgy about the idea of intense physical exercise. Fitness was something he always took for granted – a natural gift. But three months of sloth had devastated definition and stamina. It gave him a new insight into the term 'downward spiral'.

Swayne picked a plain white T-shirt off a shelf in the wardrobe. A black leather photo album fell to the floor as he did so. 'We'll be jogging in the morning,' he said, before pulling the T-shirt over his head.

Luke's attention waned. He was more interested in picking up the photo album. It lay open on a page with four photographs of Peter and David standing together outside a caravan park wearing matching navy T-shirts and shorts. They were no older than seven or eight. The cheerful smiles and arms slung around each other's shoulders in a brotherly show of affection struck Luke as strange. It wasn't an image that sprang to mind when he thought of the Swayne brothers.

'Tramore, June, 'ninety-three,' Swayne said softly. Luke handed the photo album to him. For a moment, it seemed as if they were on the verge of discussing something important. But Swayne quickly changed the subject.

'Yeah, anyway. Tomorrow, seven a.m. sharp,' he said abruptly.

Luke could sense the simultaneous fall of head and shoulders. It wasn't the right time for a heart-to-heart. 'Right, see you then,' he said softly.

Luke walked from Merrion Grove and the Swayne household with a completely altered perception of his one-time tormentor. In a sense, the tribulations he faced were trivial in comparison to the pain and loss thrust upon Peter. He had lost a brother – his only brother. Luke had ended a romance, injured a part of his body – which was now healed – and quaffed and binged his way to the brink of oblivion. All these so-called misfortunes were of his own making. He was the one who had challenged for the ball, dumped Ella, and made a pig of himself night after night.

David Swayne nailed it on the head that night in Dalkey

quarry. 'You have no idea what a real problem is.' He was right. With the unpleasant prospect of sweat and hard work around the corner, a moment to contemplate this accusation was the perfect mental wake-up call to prepare him for the pain.

REGIME

Saturday the seventh of February was the first day of Woodlawn Comprehensive's mid-term break. On Friday night Luke set his alarm clock for six-thirty a.m. and laid a tracksuit and runners out beside the radiator. It was still dark when the nagging *beep-beep-beep* of the alarm clock pierced his ears. He coiled upright like a faulty jack-in-the-box and made a jaded attempt to wipe the sleep from his eyes and yawn away his lethargy. After which he went about the business of preparing himself for the pain. A swift toilet stop to unload his bladder followed by a semi-automatic dressing procedure left him ready to rock 'n' roll with five minutes to spare.

Swayne would buzz on the intercom when he arrived. Meanwhile, Luke sat at the kitchen counter, observing the wondrous sight of a house on downtime – enjoying its peaceful slumber. The *ding-dong* of the intercom rang out at seven a.m. on the dot. Luke picked up the receiver and buzzed in his personal trainer. It seemed fitting that the addition of such a frivolous agent of entourage coincided with his move to the ivory towers of Killiney. Perhaps it was a disease he had contracted. No longer able to motivate himself, he now relied on hired help to regain his physical fitness.

'All right,' Luke said quietly, opening the front door.

Swayne dismounted from his mountain bike at the end of

the driveway and parked it neatly against the porch column. 'Breakfast time,' he said brightly.

Luke watched him walk in. He was somewhat surprised. 'Breakfast?' he replied silently.

Luke stepped back inside, closing the front door behind him. He was about to ask the question, but the sight of Swayne popping four slices of brown bread into the toaster said it all. He went to the fridge and took out the tub of Golden Olive low-fat spread, then raided the bulging fruit bowl for two hairy little critters, known as kiwi fruit.

'It's not a good idea to start a workout without something inside you. Something light,' Swayne said. He sliced the top of the kiwi fruit like someone would crack open a hard-boiled egg. Luke did likewise and tasted the juicy green innards. After a quick round of toast and a tall glass of mineral water they stepped outside to be greeted by the weasely whirl of a minor gale. There was no sign of rain, but the arctic wind cutting through them like a sharp kitchen knife provided enough hostile force for Luke to consider quitting straight away.

'Right, stretches,' Swayne said.

Luke knew the drill. When Leslie and Lofty joined the Stretford Enders and helped to mastermind the infamous five-mile jogs, they explained and demonstrated the importance of a proper warm-up routine. Swayne sat on his mountain bike while Luke stretched his groin, hamstrings and thigh muscles. He clipped a blue water bottle to the frame of the bike.

'OK, I'll be your pacemaker. Just follow me,' he said.

Luke took a deep, deep breath. He felt exhausted already, even after a simple warm-up routine. If Swayne agreed to leave, renege on his part of the bargain, Luke would happily skulk back to bed. But that was *not* about to happen. Swayne shot off down the driveway. Within seconds, he was glancing over his shoulder to check on Luke's progress.

'Why am I doing this?' Luke said with a quiet groan. He started to jog after the mountain bike and thereby put his first footstep on the long road to recovery.

A fierce, icy wind continually blasted Luke in the face. He gasped vainly for air, his lungs on fire, his legs a dead weight and weary. Surely he would black out and collapse before reaching the top of Vico Road. Swayne was twenty feet ahead of him, pumping his legs hard to maintain any sort of momentum. Unbeknown to Luke, the five-mile course his trainer had mapped out for the jog and the northerly direction they had undertaken was dominated by steep inclines. Vico Road and Dalkey Avenue, the two main stretches of road, were essentially hills. This could be seen as an inspiring challenge or downright cruelty, depending on your point of view.

'Come on,' Swayne shouted. He dropped off the pace, allowing Luke to slowly catch up with his mountain bike. This was a good time to negotiate.

'I can't do it, I can't,' Luke said, gasping desperately. His legs were barely moving and the gusts of wind pushing against him became stronger with each weary thrust forward. It was inevitable – he had reached breaking point.

Luke halted abruptly. Swayne stopped cycling. 'Get your head up,' he said calmly.

Luke's head was tucked beneath his legs.

'What are you waiting for? Come on!' Swayne shouted. Luke lifted his head. The change in tact and tone of voice was the least of his worries. He glanced at the blurred image in front of him. The road ahead was impossible.

'Come on,' Swayne said impatiently.

Somehow, Luke managed to comply. He began to move his legs again, slowly. Every single step was torture and one thought dominated his mind – stopping. 'Stop, Stop, Stop.' He could hear the word chanted in his mind like a mantra. But somehow, he closed his eyes and forged on. He allowed his brain to slip away and for a short while random thoughts began to breeze through. Gascoigne parading in an Everton jersey, Blur playing 'Tender' on *Top of the Pops*. A barrage of unconnected images occupied the empty spaces, helping him to make it through another five hundred yards. But before long the pain began to gnaw away at him. It chewed at his gut like a puppy shredding a sock. The persistent cramp in his calves became unbearable. He had no choice this time: physically he was unable to go on.

Swayne had disappeared round the corner onto Sorrento Road while Luke ground to a halt at the top of Vico Road. It was fifteen seconds before he returned.

Luke waved his hand as a white flag of surrender.

'Get going,' Swayne said coldly.

Luke couldn't raise enough breath to argue.

'Get going,' Swayne repeated forcefully.

This was the final straw. Luke summoned breath from some unknown source to retort. 'Fuck you,' he said wearily.

Swayne stood tall and stared him through. He didn't flinch a millimetre under the bile-driven abuse. 'Get – going,' he said in a slow, deliberate tone. Luke was on the verge of tears. The force of the wind continued to intensify. It was a full-blown hurricane whipping past their shoulders as they faced one another in a tense, Old West style stand-off. Swayne resembled the heartless lawman, laying down a candid ultimatum to the drifter with the unfeasibly quick-draw 'Leave town, today.'

'Wanker,' Luke coughed bitterly.

Swayne stood fast. He stared at Luke until he dropped his head and jogged on. His face was dispassionate in the scene of such abuse. But he knew the significance of his victory. A spirit bruised and broken, a soul proclaiming surrender was now, very slowly, moving forward. Luke stumbled onto Sorrento Road. Swayne did not smile. He simply placed his right foot on a bike pedal and set off after his subject. Three and a half miles to go.

The top of Castle Street, twice on Dalkey Avenue, once down Killiney Hill Road and once on Military Road. These were the points along the route when Luke broke down in exhaustion, exchanged heated words with his trainer, hurling a dictionary of abuse in his face, before struggling on. He was a rolling ball of sweat when Killiney train station appeared on the horizon like a mirage. He gasped and puffed desperately and crossed the finish line, where Swayne sat on his mountain bike. The sound of a stopwatch clicking infuriated Luke further. He shot a spiteful stare at Swayne to occupy the time it would take for him to acquire enough breath to attack verbally. In the end, the planned torrent of abuse came down to one key word.

'Dickhead,' he screamed at his tormentor. Luke limped off home. He realised this final outburst had probably burnt the last bridge which could speed him towards his career in professional football. But it was worth it, just to scream that one word into the face of Swayne – cheap at half the price. When he arrived back at the palace, he found Martina and D'Argo enjoying breakfast in the kitchen. Both were dressed for a day at the office.

'Luke,' his mother said anxiously.

Luke was in no humour to explain. He waved his hand in recognition of her greeting and slumped down the hall into his bedroom. He reeked of a pungent, sweaty aroma. But the effort involved in undressing and crawling the five yards to the shower was too much to face. An hour later, when the heat of the moment had passed by, he started to regret his continual outbursts at Swayne. Despite the torturous pain, he did manage to jog five miles. It took sixty-five minutes and seven unscheduled breaks, but he made it all the way round.

Without Swayne, Luke would have quit that first time on Vico Road, skulked back home to bed, making a quick pit stop at Foley's newsagent's for supplies, and spent the afternoon gorging himself silly. He rolled off his bed. He limped down the hall, into the kitchen and picked up the cordless phone from the kitchen counter. If he called right away and apologised, maybe they could continue with the training. Suddenly, it all came flooding back. The Fs, the Cs, the Bs, the Ws. Swayne would need his head tested to come back after what he had called him, right to his face. The invisible rain cloud appeared above. Luke slouched sadly to his room. The plan was simple. An hour of sleep, a trip to Foley's and a lifetime of regret.

Luke's plan was for an hour of sleep. It didn't quite work out that way. In fact, if it weren't for the continual *ding-dong* of the intercom, he would have slept right through until Sunday morning. He struggled to his feet and walked down the hall into the kitchen.

'Hello,' he slurred sleepily into the intercom.

'It's me,' Swayne replied.

Luke was shocked. He hit the button to open the security gates and squinted at the digital clock on the microwave to check the time. Quarter past one. The knock on the front door followed a few seconds later. It was a tricky moment for him. He searched his mind desperately for the right phrase of apology. 'Sorry I called you a wanker' just didn't seem to cut it. In the end, there was no need for words.

'Drink this,' Swayne said. He handed Luke a bottle of Lucozade Sport as soon as he walked through the front door. Luke held the bottle in his hand a while, glancing suspiciously at the orange liquid. Was there a foreign substance in the mix that would square things up?

'How do your calves feel?' Swayne said.

'Fine,' Luke replied. He studied his trainer's expression carefully. There was no sign of resentment or hurt in his eyes. No emotion whatsoever. Luke opened the bottle of Lucozade Sport and sank half of it in one go.

'Have you got a back garden?' Swayne asked.

'Erm, yeah,' Luke replied.

'Is there much of a lawn?'

Luke simply nodded his head this time. Swayne reached into his backpack and pulled something out. It was a skipping rope. 'When you're ready,' he said.

The beautiful backdrop of Killiney Bay proved helpful to Luke as he skipped. It gave him something to concentrate upon when the aches and spasms of cramp crept up his legs. Swayne sat behind him, stopwatch in hand.

'Come on, pick up the pace,' he said firmly. Luke did so. He wasn't much of a skipper, but the fact he wasn't running felt like a gift from God. Exercises on the spot somehow seemed less painful. The sound of 'Lifting Me Higher' by Jackie Wilson set the tempo. Swayne had suggested an upbeat musical soundtrack to help maintain the right energy level. He was in charge of the stereo.

'Ten more minutes,' he announced.

Luke's calves were on fire. He could feel the secretions bond his T-shirt to his back and the droplets of sweat stream down his temples onto his eyelids. 'Just a little longer, just a little longer,' he chanted to himself. The ten minutes crawled along like a glacier during an ice age. But he battled through to the end and slumped onto his knees with the rope tangled round his ankles.

Swayne switched off the stereo, cutting off 'A Town Called Malice' in its prime. He walked over to Luke and handed him the bottle of Lucozade Sport, now full to the brim with mineral water.

'I've made lunch for you,' Swayne said. 'See you at seven o'clock.'

Luke looked up at him. 'What?' he gasped.

Swayne was halfway through the back door. He turned to explain. 'I'll meet you down on the beach,' he said.

'Swimming?' Luke said dramatically. Swayne nodded. He continued inside the house, closing the door behind him. Luke turned onto his side. He caught a glimpse of the heaving swirl below. Swimming in the Irish Sea in the middle of February. What had he done to deserve this fate? When he limped into the kitchen and saw his lunch laid out on the counter, he knew exactly what he had done to deserve it. A tuna, tomato and cucumber sandwich, low-fat strawberry yoghurt, an apple, a pear and a glass of orange juice. There was a yellow post-it attached to the plate.

DO NOT EAT AFTER LUNCH!!!

Luke munched the apple. It wouldn't be a problem. He could hardly find the energy to keep his eyelids separated, let alone binge. He slid a tray beneath his lunch-time bounty and retired to his bedroom.

It was definitely taking its toll. Luke fell asleep again in the afternoon. He woke at quarter past seven, thanks to the incessant *drring-drring* of the phone. After perfecting his zombie walk down the hall, he picked up the receiver and groaned.

'Yeah, yeah. I'll be down in five minutes,' Luke said sleepily. There was no one else in the palace. He went back to his bedroom, packed a beach towel and a pair of Everton shorts into his kit bag and set off. On the way down the driveway, he saw the security gates roll back and the super-high beam of the Cherokee's headlights coming towards him. D'Argo halted the Jeep at Martina's behest.

'Where are you off to now?' she said.

'Beach, swim,' Luke replied, unable to muster any enthusiasm for conversation.

Martina was anxious to ask her usual twenty questions. Who, what, when, where, how, so on, so forth. But it was obvious her son needed to conserve what little energy remained within his jaded bones. 'Be careful,' she said.

Luke found himself staring at D'Argo before the Jeep drove on down the driveway. He didn't bother to utter a single word. It was amazing how little the man bothered with him. They were, after all, living under the same roof. But the effort involved in a simple hello or goodbye was beyond him. When Luke reached Killiney beach he found it cloaked in a beautiful darkness. Swayne stood on the pebbly underfoot in anticipation, his kit bag beside his left ankle. They were the only souls along the lonely stretch of shore.

'Let me guess, Wales and back,' Luke said dryly. It was difficult to be certain in the darkness, but he sensed a smile appear on Swayne's face.

'Have you eaten?' he said.

Luke shook his head. The gale-force winds of the morning and afternoon had blown themselves out. All that remained for the evening was a gentle breeze. Swayne stripped into his Speedos, Luke did likewise.

'Follow me,' Swayne said. They walked slowly to the shore. A wave came crashing down at Luke's feet with a foaming gush. The icy liquid jabbed at his skin.

'Jesus,' he said, letting out a high-pitched squeal of shock.

Swayne looked at him. 'Stay close by,' he said.

Luke shivered. Swayne waded out into the water as if paddling his feet on a scorching July afternoon. Luke decided to return to basics. He took three deep lungfuls for courage before dashing out to Swayne's side. His cowardly squeals of agony eventually faded. The two boys swam out to sea side by side. After two minutes in the water Luke felt a strange rejuvenation. Energy he was adamant no longer existed sprang forth from his arms and legs as he kicked and stroked forward. Each time he twisted his neck topside to suck in oxygen, it propelled him onward. For twenty-five minutes they matched each other stroke for stroke. It was only then that Luke found it hard to keep pace with Swayne. They had been in the water for a long time, swimming the breadth of Killiney beach from the train station to Hawk Cliff.

'Swayne,' Luke said loudly, 'how much longer?'

Swayne suspended his stroke and turned in the water. 'Back to the station and out,' he replied.

Luke took another deep breath and went back to work on his butterfly stroke. He could make out the glare of the orange streetlamps illuminating the station off in the distance, another hundred yards or so to go. Swayne was a powerful swimmer and could have kept up the relentless pace he set over the last twenty-five minutes. But instead, he slowed down and stayed by Luke's side all the way to the shore.

'Get dried off,' Swayne said, tossing Luke his towel. An aggregate of one hundred and fifty-seven minutes' physical exercise caught up with him when they left the water. He found it hard standing up straight, drying his skin with the towel, even keeping his eyelids apart.

'Come on, get dressed,' Swayne insisted. 'You'll catch your death.' Luke snapped out of his daze. He rubbed his hair, back, arms and legs before removing his shorts. Swayne was already dressing.

'How long were we out there?' Luke asked.

'Fifty minutes,' Swayne replied quickly. It took them five minutes to get dressed. Luke noticed how little they said to one another in between. Even that morning and afternoon, their only real conversations involved an exchange of taunts and insults. When they were both ready to leave, Swayne tossed a bottle of Ballygowan mineral water to Luke.

'Come on,' he said. 'I'm starving.' Luke tried to keep pace behind his trainer as they walked from the beach. He didn't share his appetite for food. The only thing he wanted to do was sleep for a month.

Back in D'Argo's palace, Luke and Swayne headed straight for his bedroom. Martina ambushed them in the hallway: she was dressed for a night out.

'Everything OK?' she said. Luke frowned. What was that supposed to mean?

Martina did cringe slightly at her innocuous faux pas. She was desperate to know what was going on but couldn't find a reasonable excuse to ask nosy questions. 'I mean, did you have a nice swim?' she added, trying to cover up her embarrassment.

'Yeah, super,' Luke replied vacantly. He and Swayne went into his bedroom and shut the world outside. Martina hung on in the hall for a moment, before walking away to the kitchen. Luke crashed onto his bed in a state of total exhaustion while Swayne pulled out the chair beneath the computer table and placed his kit bag on it. He unzipped the bag and pulled out a bottle of baby oil and a can of Ralgex.

'Have you got a clean towel?' Swayne said.

Luke struggled to pull himself upright. 'Why?' he asked.

'I'm going to give you a massage.'

Over the past few days, Luke had become accustomed to some rather peculiar developments in his life. Peter Swayne becoming a companion, confidant and personal trainer were all million-to-one shots. But this . . . this was plain bizarre. Before he could point out the glut of homosexual connotations involved in one teenage boy massaging the other, Swayne explained the method behind his madness.

'Today is day one. We've got fifty-five more days of intense cardiovascular training to go. If you're to last that long, you'll need to take extra special care of your muscles – especially those on your legs and the small of your back. A massage is the best way to combat fatigue and injury.'

It was a top-notch explanation, but Luke couldn't shake the overall gayness of the whole affair from his mind.

'Stop acting like a kid,' Swayne said impatiently. Luke straightened his shoulders. Maturity was something he prided himself on. He hopped off his bed and walked over to the Sliderobe. He picked out a fresh pair of shorts and a clean white towel.

The groan of relaxation Luke strangled in his throat upon the laying on of Swayne's healing hands was enormous. Each expert rub of his aching muscles brought relief and unspeakable alleviation. The distinct smell of Ralgex filled the air. Luke felt the burning grip of the spray as it attached itself to his legs, back and shoulders.

'Right, all done,' Swayne announced.

Luke sprang from the mattress like a squirrel jumping from a tree. If the truth be known, he wanted to sink off to sleep with Swayne gently massaging his back. But this kind of reaction to the end of the massage could have posed a serious question about his sexuality. After all, he was single, a teenager and prone to impulsive acts of confusion. Luke was on his feet in an instant, bobbing and weaving about his bedroom like a middleweight boxer preparing for a world title fight.

Swayne watched him with a microscopic smirk. 'Dinner time,' he said.

Making full use of the supplies they had bought the day before, Swayne prepared a healthy stir-fry chicken dish with egg noodles. By the time he served it, Luke had fallen asleep in front of the TV. It was quarter to nine. Instead of waking him, he decided to leave the plate on the kitchen counter and quietly make his way outside. Sunday would see a repeat of the same routine. Jog in the morning, skip in the afternoon, swim in the evening. The key word was routine: once it was established, it would be difficult to destroy.

THE FIRST WEEK

Sunday was a nightmare, every single step of the way. Jogging five miles was the same sinuous struggle as the day before. Insults were again hurled at Peter Swayne as he forced Luke on through the pain barrier. By the time they reached the start/finish point at Killiney train station, Luke had come to a decision.

'I'm finished. I've had enough,' he said fiercely.

Swayne allowed him to storm off. But at one o'clock, the intercom *ding-donged* and he stood outside the security gates with a skipping rope and a bottle of Lucozade Sport. Ten minutes into the skip, when his left lung seemed to collapse inside his chest, Luke flung the skipping rope over the back garden wall. It fell sixty feet to the bottom of Killiney Hill.

'Checkmate,' he said to Swayne. He was wrong. Luke had no get-out clause while Peter Swayne was about. Instead of using a rope, he was forced to skip 'freestyle'. Despite the numerous complaints he made about feeling foolish, Swayne forced him to jump up and down, twisting his arms as if he held a rope, until he had completed the thirty-minute session.

'Next time, hold onto the rope. You won't feel half as foolish,' Swayne said before leaving D'Argo's palace that afternoon. Luke shoved a mid-digit into the air.

The evening swim was the only part of the ruthless regime Luke enjoyed. The large body of water bore the brunt of the burden. Once he acclimatised to the frigid temperature, he found the thirty-minute jaunt from the station to Hawk Cliff and back again relaxing. But Swayne was still there to remind him of the reason.

'Stay with me. Don't slacken,' he would say, as he powered through the water. Luke's response would be to quietly insult his trainer or openly question his sexuality while working all four limbs overtime to lift the tempo. This kind of abuse didn't seem to bother Swayne. The only time he became agitated was when Luke slowed down. After the swim and massage, Swayne cooked dinner. Roasted chicken breasts, skinless of course, boiled potatoes and a side salad.

Luke examined the plate doubtfully. 'Is this it?' he said.

Swayne chewed a piece of chicken. 'For the time being,' he replied.

Luke didn't catch the hidden meaning. He sighed sadly before tucking into his dinner. Dieting and healthy eating was an alien act to him. He had always eaten whatever he liked, crisps, chocolate, chips, etc., and stayed the same – slim. Binge eating was something he could handle.

'If you stick to this diet for eight weeks, you'll be two stone lighter, guaranteed,' Swayne said out of the blue.

Luke looked up at him.

'Once you've regained your fitness, you can go back to scoffing junk food,' Swayne added. This sounded more like it. It no longer resembled a life sentence of healthy eating, fruit and vegetables and a balanced diet. Just an eight-week nightmare of restraint. Luke could handle eight weeks.

The following five days of February felt like a spell inside a pressure cooker to Luke. Each day, he attempted to raise his tired bones to the challenge of an exhausting five-mile slog.

But each day, he would barely make it past the corner of Vico Road without grinding to a halt. His breathless pleas for mercy would fall upon the deaf ears of Swayne. Their relationship developed accordingly – Luke shouted and screamed abuse, Swayne refused to let him quit. The love-hate dynamic created a simple state of mind for both trainer and trainee.

Quitting would not be tolerated.

Swayne was beginning to resemble an Italian man-marker. Everywhere Luke went, he followed. From morning till evening, Peter Swayne was lurking in the shadows to keep him on his toes. But exercise wasn't his only concern. He kept a close eye on Luke's diet, preparing each meal, searching his bedroom for hidden junk stashes, encouraging him to drink mineral water throughout the day. He was a relentless figure in the battle of the bulge.

But inside the pressure cooker an explosion was imminent. In spite of all the exercise, all the sweat and effort, Luke was becoming increasingly frustrated by his lack of progress. He didn't feel any fitter on Thursday than he had done first thing Saturday morning, even with the diligent, superhuman efforts of Peter Swayne. One thought was foremost in Luke's mind – quitting. On Friday morning, he wheezed in pain as he reached the lower part of Sorrento Road. A new, overwhelming strain of determination persuaded him to submit to the negativity festering in his mind. Swayne continued to cycle up the road. It was a while before he glanced behind him. To his surprise, not only had Luke stopped jogging, he had also turned round and started to walk home.

Swayne cycled back to question him. 'What are you doing?' he shouted angrily.

Luke continued walking, refusing to enter into a pep-talk style debate. Swayne dismounted his bike and cut across his path. He stopped him with physical force. A precise but gentle shove to the chest.

'I said, what are you doing?'

Luke stopped. He stared Swayne straight in the eye while panting heavily. 'Look, thanks for everything, OK. But I've had enough. I don't care about football any more. I just want to go home,' he explained candidly.

Luke waited for it. But Swayne stayed silent, he had no defence against such logical reasoning. Luke still expected some kind of verbal reply. But if it didn't arrive in the next ten seconds, he was on his way.

'This is day seven,' Swayne said.

'So?' Luke replied. 'What difference does that make?'

Swayne reached out a hand to Luke's sweater and grabbed a roll of flab.

'Get your hands off me,' Luke shouted aggressively. He tried to retreat, but Swayne held on tightly. They stared at one another intensely.

'It took you three months to get yourself into this mess. It'll take you at least two to get out of it,' Swayne said. He released the roll of flab. His eyes softened. 'But you will get out of it,' he added.

Luke was disgusted with himself. Somehow, he had become involved in a process of negotiation. Two minutes beforehand he was officially quitting, but now the decision was back in the balance. He needed some kind of rational argument. An exceptional point entered his head.

'Why do I feel worse now than I did last Saturday?' he said frankly.

Swayne smiled. 'It gets easier,' he said. 'But it'll never be easy.'

Without another word, Swayne walked over to his mountain bike and picked it up off the ground. Luke took several deep breaths to steel himself for the challenge of Sorrento Road. He began jogging before Swayne was cycling. Upon passing him, he said, 'I really hate you.'

Swayne watched Luke move past him. He seemed to tackle the steep incline of Sorrento Road with a fresh resolve and gritty tenacity. A bright smile appeared on Swayne's face. He mounted his bike and pedalled hard to catch and overtake his young charge.

After the massage on Friday evening Luke faced his first moment of truth. He watched Swayne walk into the en suite bathroom and retrieve the scales. He placed them on the floor in front of Luke and invited him to step up.

Luke hesitated.

'Come on,' Swayne said.

Luke remained reluctant. He wanted some magic words of encouragement. But Swayne had used up the day's quota quelling the Sorrento Road insurrection. He finally displayed that famous short fuse.

'Come on, Luke. Stop acting like a woman,' Swayne said rudely.

Luke stepped onto the scales but didn't dare look down. Swayne arched his own neck towards the floor to check what progress had been made in seven days. He smiled.

'What does it say?' Luke asked anxiously.

Swayne didn't reply. He decided to leave him to find out for himself. Luke sighed in frustration. It could be nothing but bad news, the shock of which had sent Swayne into a speechless slump. Slowly he opened his eyes and peered down.

'What?' Luke said in delight. The needle was holding steady halfway between seventy-two and seventy-three kilos. The mathematical calculation escaped him. He had to turn to Swayne for confirmation.

'Eight pounds. Over half a stone,' he said happily.

For the first time in three months Luke Farrell could honestly claim to be happy. He squeezed his fist in celebration and hopped off the scales. Swayne opened his green notebook and jotted down the particulars. He noticed the joyous spring in Luke's step.

'That's a great start,' Swayne said. 'But just remember, it's only a start.'

The words of warning were heeded by Luke. He had no intention of falling back into the hole. He might only be a few inches off the floor of the pit of despair, but it had given him fresh appetite for the climb. He sat down on his bed, silently celebrating his week of triumph by examining his flabby frame. His shameful spare tyre was diminishing. Swayne busied himself with his customary search of the bedroom for junk food. It wasn't a sign of mistrust, just another ritual to help embed the routine in Luke's mind.

'Right, I'll see you in the morning,' Swayne said.

'Oh, OK,' Luke replied. He walked with Swayne down the hall to the front door. Along the way he wanted to ask him to stay around for some mode of celebration. A carrot stick or two, ten victory push-ups. But instead, he let him leave D'Argo's palace without another word.

Luke had plans for Saturday that didn't involve a run up Sorrento Road or a swim to Hawk Cliff. The time had come for him to start living up to his part of the bargain – although the thought of reuniting Swayne with the blonde witch Cecilia didn't seem the best way of expressing his gratitude. However, it was what Swayne wanted from him. And as Mrs Hendy would often say, 'Each to his own.'

Model Citizens

The idea had been gestating in Luke's mind for the past week of pain. At times, his sole desire was to execute unspeakable acts of violence against Swayne that would certainly have jeopardised the viability of his scheme. But now that the painful return to exercise was becoming more manageable by the day, he set about putting the wheels in motion. After the five-mile jog on Saturday morning, he sat down on the wall of the Killiney Court Hotel car park and glugged his bottle of water.

Swayne scribbled something in his green notepad. It gave Luke an opportunity to test the water.

'Are you busy after lunch?' he said.

Swayne looked up from his notepad. 'Why?' he replied cautiously, expecting to hear some pitiful excuse to skip the evening swim.

'There's somewhere we need to go,' Luke said cryptically. He stood up and walked up Station Road.

Swayne followed on his mountain bike. When he reached Luke's side he said with a straight face, 'After the skip?'

Luke shook his head in derision. 'Yes, after the skip.'

After the lunch-time skipping session Swayne was so adamant they complete, Luke had a quick shower and changed into some regular, non-exercising type clothing. He refused to divulge their destination despite rigorous questioning from an apprehensive Swayne.

'We're not gonna miss the evening swim, are we?' he said anxiously.

Luke closed his eyes and groaned. The job of personal trainer and unrelenting taskmaster had gone to Swayne's head. He was becoming obsessed with schedules. 'No, we'll be back in plenty of time,' Luke assured him.

'So where are we going then?' Swayne demanded.

'Shopping,' Luke replied. He continued down Station Road towards Killiney train station. A short trip into town would be the perfect setting to pitch his ingenious plan to win back the heart of Cecilia Giles. The right setting was essential if Swayne was to go along with Luke's unorthodox approach. And the right setting was St Stephen's Green shopping centre.

Swayne followed Luke closely along a bustling Grafton Street. He still had no idea where they were going, and despite an unending stream of questions to crowbar the location from Luke, he remained in the dark.

'Right, here we are,' Luke said. He and Swayne stopped at the top of Grafton Street; they both looked across at the main entrance of St Stephen's Green shopping centre.

'The shopping centre?' Swayne said doubtfully.

Luke nodded. Although the pedestrian walk sign remained red, he and a host of Saturday afternoon shoppers dispensed with the law and walked straight across the road. Swayne stalled, waiting with a small minority of law-abiding folk for the sign to turn green. The thumping bass of some trashy dance track pounded the walls and windows of the shopping centre. A large crowd swelled in the aisles and walkways, concentrating their attention on the makeshift marquee posted in the centre of the ground floor.

'What is all this?' Swayne said loudly.

Luke snaked his way forward, through the tightly packed throng, to gain a better view. Swayne trailed after him, ten seconds or so behind. When he caught up, his jaw dropped in horror.

'Come on, let's go,' he said firmly.

Luke heard the request, but his eyes were dazzled and his limbs paralysed by the fluid movement of two tall blonde girls in bikinis, striding towards him in unison like some fantastic wet dream.

'Come on,' Swayne shouted, dragging Luke from his vision forcefully.

'Relax. I'm coming,' he replied angrily.

Swayne barged his way back through the crowd, away from the front of the catwalk to the relative privacy of a barren Golden Discs shop floor. He eyeballed Luke irately and demanded an explanation. 'Is this some kind of joke?' he said sharply.

Luke felt like a giggle. His face was cocked in a snide smirk before he realised how ignorant and rude a reaction it was. Swayne was obviously upset and didn't deserve to be treated in such an inconsiderate manner.

'No, it's not a joke,' Luke said sincerely. 'It's part of my plan.'

Swayne softened. This was the first mention of a plan. Even this tiny taster filled him with excitement. He was anxious to find out more. 'What is your plan?' he said.

Luke glanced upward. He noticed a glut of empty spaces along the second floor mezzanine. It was up there, elevated from the main body of the crowd, where they would find the seclusion they needed.

'Let's take a walk,' he said confidently.

Swayne and Luke stood on the second floor mezzanine. They had a bird's-eye view of the fashion show below, without the fear of discovery. When she finally appeared on stage, Swayne's heart melted. Luke could hear the barely disguised sigh and the eyes turning to mush. Cecilia was 'wearing', if you could call it that, a tattered silver dress with randomly cut holes in the fabric that sported a serrated hem line. Luke studied her carefully. Suddenly, he understood Tonka's reluctance to tear up the phone number. The physical attraction was easy to comprehend. But Swayne had suffered her erratic nature for nine years. She was a self-serving minx, always looking out for number one.

'Is that thing made of tin-foil?' Luke quipped.

Swayne was in a trance. Even when Cecilia disappeared from the catwalk, he found it impossible to tear his gaze away. It was a sad state of affairs.

'You want to win her back?' Luke said sharply.

Swayne turned his head instantly. Luke stared at him with a confident smile. He knew exactly how to win Cecilia back. But he also knew it was a short-term solution. When the dust settled on his little scheme, she would soon grow weary of her new toy and look elsewhere for that instant fix of excitement.

'Before I tell you what you have to do, I need to explain to you why you have to do it,' Luke said.

Swayne didn't understand. But he gestured for Luke to continue with a nod of his head.

'I need to ask you some questions,' he said.

'Yeah, go on,' Swayne replied.

Luke had been devising this simple yes/no answer quiz for the best part of two weeks. It summed up the choices available to Swayne perfectly. All the answers would end in N-O.

'Can you sing?' he said.

Swayne looked puzzled. 'No,' he replied.

'Can you act?' Luke said.

Swayne frowned. 'No,' he replied impatiently.

'Can you play football?' Luke continued. 'Skilfully.'

Swayne was losing patience. 'What's that supposed to mean?' he snapped.

'Answer the question,' Luke insisted.

Swayne sighed. 'No,' he said theatrically.

'Have you any interest in photography or fashion design?' Luke said.

Swayne stared at him, trying to uncover a snide attempt at humour. But Luke held a serious expression with ease. This was no laughing matter. Swayne finally conceded the point. This quiz was serious.

'No,' he said quietly.

Luke leaned over the mezzanine banister rail and glanced at the catwalk below. The female models were off the stage and their male counterparts were strutting their stuff two by two. It was the most exquisite timing possible.

'You can't sing, act, play football. You have no interest in fashion design or photography,' Luke said.

'Yeah, so what?' Swayne replied abruptly.

Luke turned towards him and threw his cards on the table. 'Then you'll have to become a model,' he said bluntly.

Swayne was not amused. He folded his arms across his chest and frowned the frown of all time. This was *Guinness Book of Records* style frowning. But to his surprise, Luke kept a straight face and stared right back at him. Eventually, he turned his head to observe the fashion show below, but he looked back moments later – inviting Swayne to come and inspect his future. Tentatively, he did so.

'Just hear me out, OK?' Luke said. 'If you want Cecilia to

get excited about you again, the key word is re-invention.'

Swayne noticed one chiselled specimen sporting a pair of ridiculous black leather trousers. He gulped anxiously. 'Why a model?' he pleaded.

Luke shrugged his shoulders and considered the question mindfully. 'Picture this: Cecilia opens a fashion mag and sees you modelling expensive designer sweaters. Cecilia turns up at a fashion show and sees you heading towards the men's dressing room. Four little words, my friend: putty in your hands.'

Luke smiled a reassuring smile, but Swayne was still undecided. He glanced back down at the pouting beefcakes. It didn't look like rocket science, but surely it couldn't be that simple.

'What – what makes you think I can do that?' Swayne said.

Luke didn't dare look him in the eye while listing the reasons. This was a predetermined act. A daily massage for the cause of physical fitness was one thing. Complimenting teenage boys on their looks and physique was quite another.

Luke took a deep breath. 'You're tall . . . well-built,' he said, but couldn't help pausing . . . 'Good looking,' he added inanely.

Luke concentrated hard on the catwalk below. Swayne gave an uneasy shuffle. He felt thoroughly conflicted. It was nice to be complimented, but not by a boy. Especially one you massage on a daily basis.

'Look, if you want her back, this is your best shot,' Luke said gruffly.

Swayne took another look at the catwalk below. It was an outlandish scheme to win back his girlfriend. But deep down, he knew it would work on Cecilia. To see him in such an exotic, exciting light could be the kick-start they needed.

Instead of looking down on him, perhaps she could see him as an equal.

'All right, I'll do it,' he said quietly.

Luke smiled. 'Time for a swim, I think,' he said brightly.

The two boys left the shopping centre together.

Oɴᴇ Lᴀsᴛ Kɪᴄᴋ ɪɴ ᴛʜᴇ Tᴇᴇᴛʜ

Luke waited until Swayne had left D'Argo's palace on Sunday evening before beginning his research. He sat down at his computer table and put to use the skills of sloth he had developed from November to January. The Internet had become a second home during his period of physical inactivity. Mostly, he would check out different chat rooms and porn sites, but he did know his way round the glut of information available. His key-word search started off with modelling.

'Jesus,' Luke said in amazement. Two million matches for the word 'modelling'. It was time to narrow down the scope a little.

'How to become a male model,' he mumbled as he typed. When he hit the return key, the immediate crackle of the hard drive going about its work like a drone bumble bee gave him a sense of optimism. If it couldn't be found on the Internet, it couldn't be found.

'Bingo,' Luke said quietly. His key-word search had delivered one hundred and eighty-six matches. But top of the tree was an exact word-for-word site, entitled, 'How to become a male model'. Luke double clicked on the address. Moments later, it presented him with a picture of a blond beefcake in a white Armani suit. The slogan 'WELCOME TO MY WORLD' was slung across the top of the picture.

Some American boob called Jay Actenberg, a professional model for some fifteen years, had committed to paper an 'everything you need to know' guide to becoming a male model. His credentials were impressive. He had featured in several advertising campaigns: Levi's, Gillette, Pringles, etc. He had modelled for the top fashion houses on the runways of New York, Milan, Paris and London. And since his retirement, Jay had begun teaching a course at UCLA about the pitfalls of the industry. This led to numerous appearances on US talk shows – *Oprah*, *Jenny Jones* and *Ricki Lake*. Jay Actenberg knew his stuff.

Luke noticed the message at the bottom of the website. 'Please feel free to download,' it said, referring to Jay's industry bible.

'Ta very much, Jay,' Luke said happily. He began downloading the file to his hard drive. It was over four hundred k in size and the estimated download time was fifteen minutes. To kill some time, Luke decided to check out a few Irish modelling agencies. Image Inc., which claimed to be the largest, had a somewhat skimpy website. However, one detail of note was an open advertisement seeking first-time models to appear at the Spring Show in the RDS.

'Interesting,' Luke murmured.

Image Inc. was Cecilia's agency. He quickly put two and two together and came up with 'happy ever after'. Luke fished a blue Bic biro from the top drawer of the computer table and jotted down the address for Image Inc. in Dublin. Swayne had left his green notepad in the drawer. Luke resisted the urge to spy on the scribbles inside and instead deposited the notepad in his schoolbag beside the table. He held the address up to the illuminating light of the screen and smiled confidently. This plan was shaping up nicely. He returned his attention to the screen. He went back to Actenberg's page and checked on the download. Four minutes remaining.

Luke puffed out a weary sigh. Tomorrow he would return to Woodlawn Comprehensive after their mid-term break. It was eight days since Swayne began tormenting him up the steep slope to physical fitness. He still found himself struggling for air each step of the jog. The skipping was murder on his arms and his calf muscles and the swimming squeezed his lungs to bursting point. But the important steps forward had been taken. There was no going back.

'I know,' Luke said to himself in excitement. The download was almost complete. In the meantime he navigated his way to the Preston North End Teamtalk site to check the latest info on his soon-to-be employers. Michael Turner had kept in close contact, phoning and sending him an e-mail each week with words of encouragement and general info regarding the results of the youth team in the Lancashire league. The thought of facing Michael Turner again usually brought a ghostly shiver down his spine. But in light of the positive steps he had taken over the past eight days, 10 April could not come fast enough. That was until the Teamtalk page came up on his screen.

Luke didn't know what to do. He stared at the headline in stunned silence.

GREGORY SACKED!!!

Following yesterday's 5–1 home defeat to WBA, the directors of Preston North End held an emergency board meeting and decided to terminate the contracts of manager George Gregory and his entire backroom staff.

This decision comes after a run of seven defeats in nine league games and a humiliating third-round FA Cup exit at the hands of lowly conference side, Yeovil Town. Chairman Robert Tucker made a statement quoting 'lack of direction' and 'tactical naivety' as the main reasons for their decision to sack one-time golden boy Gregory.

Speculation concerning Gregory's replacement points directly to former Liverpool manager, Roy Evans, who has been seen at a number of Preston games recently. It is thought Evans will take the reins in the next few days and set about restructuring the reserve and youth team set-ups with his own staff, including former assistant Doug Livermore, physio Mark Leather and the surprise appointment of Ian Rush and Gary Gillespie as youth team coaches.

It was the final straw. Luke knew the words on the screen signalled the end of his involvement with Preston North End. 'Luke who?' Ian Rush would say as he flicked through the files in his new office. Football is a cruel game, not one overflowing with loyalty and sentiment.

Luke pulled open the bottom drawer on the computer table. He retrieved the contract Michael Turner had presented to him in October with a sincere promise. Fate had now intervened on two separate occasions to scupper any chance of his dream becoming a reality. It was a shattering blow, a knockout punch if ever there was one. He tried to stay upbeat. Eight pounds lost, fitness returning, scouts coming to see him play on 10 April. It was all true, but it meant nothing. A nasty notion had crawled inside his head and spread a putrid cancer. 'No matter what you do, it'll always end in defeat. You're a born loser, just like your father.' A tear rolled down his cheek. The little remaining resolve he had collapsed in dramatic fashion. There was only one logical course of action left to pursue.

Swayne was halfway home when he realised the green notepad was not in transit. He turned his mountain bike round immediately and started back to D'Argo's palace. It was risky leaving the contents of the notepad open to Luke Farrell's eyes. Such sensitive information concerning his own rehabilitation could have detrimental effects. When he reached the security gates, a dark saloon car was pulling out of the driveway. Swayne took advantage of the opening and continued inside. He parked his mountain bike by the side of the porch and rang the doorbell. There was no immediate answer.

Swayne glanced at his watch. Ten past nine. Surely Luke wasn't in bed. A second ring of the doorbell was in order. The sinister whistle of the breeze behind him forced Swayne to shuffle slightly. He was beginning to sense something bad in the air. Finally, Luke opened the door. Guilt was plastered across his face.

'I left my notepad behind,' Swayne said, stepping inside the front door without invitation. Luke scrambled after him, desperate to hide his shame. He was too late. Swayne had already copped an eyeful as he passed by the hall. Sighting the heaped plate on the kitchen counter wasn't necessary – the distinctive aroma carried for miles.

'What's this?' he said quietly.

Luke sighed. 'A curry – what does it look like?' he replied sarcastically, moving past Swayne to be with his comfort food.

Luke kept his head bowed. He was well aware of Swayne's

on-going stare of disapproval. He couldn't find the courage to face him.

'I know, all right. I know,' Luke pleaded.

Swayne remained silent until Luke finally found the guts to look him in the eye.

'What do you know?' he said sharply.

Luke fumbled to find the words. He didn't have the energy to justify his submission. All he wanted was food and privacy. Swayne wasn't about to provide these privileges without an excellent explanation.

'It's over, OK. All this dieting, all this training. None of it matters,' Luke said.

'Why?' Swayne replied quickly.

Luke didn't even want to think about it. He sighed deeply. 'Michael Turner got the bullet,' he said.

This was explanation enough. Enough for Luke, but not for Swayne. He groaned in frustration before elaborating on the gloomy situation.

'Look, I had a two-year contract with Preston. All I had to do was prove my fitness,' Luke said. 'But when a manager gets the chop, everything he had planned gets chopped as well, including me.'

This should have been reason enough to sabotage a week of hard work and effort. Swayne stood motionless, watching Luke like a scornful schoolteacher. It was an action that drove him insane. A verbal reply would have speeded up the entire process and saved him from soggy chips. He prompted a reply.

'Come on. Get on with your pep talk,' Luke snapped.

Swayne shrugged his shoulders. 'What's the point?' he said bleakly.

Luke found himself surprised by the reply. His defensive shield dropped down a notch or two and he ventured a quiet question. 'What do you mean?' he asked.

Swayne took a seat at the kitchen counter and faced Luke in a passive manner. 'I can't keep coming up with reasons for you to stick at it. If you're determined to destroy all our hard work, there's nothing I can do to stop you.'

Luke gulped. His justification was gone. All the usual reasons to gorge himself silly no longer applied. At that precise moment, he could lay no blame at the door of the harsh, cruel world. Tonka, Ella, Jerome, the Enders, D'Argo, Martina, etc. etc. His ability to pin misfortune on specific targets who made his life a misery was the key to comfort eating. Food was the alternative to the callous cast of characters who surrounded him and made it their life's work for him to be unhappy.

Luke no longer had that airbag.

'If you eat that curry, you'll hurt yourself, no one else,' Swayne said.

Luke focused on him again. The heat of the plate on the palm of his hand was a reminder of what was at stake. Eight days in, the hardest eight days of his life. He couldn't throw it all away in a moment of weakness. Swayne sensed the change in his expression. His conviction to give into temptation was waning. It was time to follow up his last comment.

'If you get past this moment, you're three-quarters way home.'

Luke wanted to believe in these words. It was the kind of shimmering light in the distance that made it possible to survive what was surely his lowest ebb.

'And I'll help you all the way,' Swayne said softly.

Luke stared at him. The moment had passed. The cancer that corrupted his mind was eradicated. He could now face the pain. Swayne watched Luke walk to the kitchen sink. He opened the cupboard beneath and gently tipped the contents of the plate into the white plastic bin. A puff of starchy vapour crawled towards the ceiling. Luke and Swayne stood in silence. There was nothing left to say.

Jay Actenberg's Words of Wisdom

Luke spent one whole week studying the book written by former beefcake Jay Actenberg. The wonderfully lucid text was littered with helpful tips on grooming, physical fitness, posing techniques and catwalk styles. But the one phrase Jay liked to hammer into the heads of his budding followers like a Buddhist mantra was: Build a portfolio. Luke had undertaken such a task, piecing together the various components necessary to produce a slick, professional series of shots. But like a famous Chinese philosopher once said, 'First learn to walk, then you can worry about flying.'

'Are you sure we're alone?' Swayne whispered. His words echoed loudly across the vast chasm of the school gymnasium. Luke closed the gym door behind him and threw his schoolbag on a stack of plastic chairs beside the light switches before walking across to a row of tables.

'Relax. Everyone has a half day,' he replied.

Swayne stood by the door nervously. He had prepared himself for some peculiar requests when he agreed to go ahead with Luke's kooky plan, but this was beginning to seem more like an extravagant practical joke.

'Give us a hand,' Luke said. He was standing on the opposite side of the gymnasium waiting at one end of a table. Swayne reluctantly walked over to join him and help carry the table to the edge of a wall. Although Luke refused to explain, it was clear to Swayne they were building some sort of structure. They lined up the tables two by two, stretching eight tables long into the centre of the vast hall.

'Is this a catwalk?' Swayne said when they had finished.

Luke turned to him, bemused. 'Of course it's a catwalk,' he replied. He sighed quietly before walking back to his schoolbag. He produced a small portable stereo and a skipping rope. Synergy was the key word. While Swayne was learning to walk, Luke could be improving his fitness. After a second week of diet and training, he had lost a further three pounds. That was eleven in total, three short of a stone.

'Right. I've been reading this bloke's book. He's pretty much the Maradona of male models,' Luke said. He jumped onto the makeshift stage and walked to the wall. He had positioned the first two tables for convenient access to a power socket. He plugged in his portable stereo and cued up the practice tape, labelled 'Satisfaction One'.

'Right,' Luke said, after turning to face Swayne, who stood on the gym floor below.

'Jay Actenberg suggests the Rolling Stones' "Satisfaction" as a good practice tune to walk to. Not for the beat, just for the attitude. Cool, controlled, just the right side of arrogant.'

Luke crouched down and pressed play on the stereo. As the timeless guitar riff cut across the empty gymnasium, he advised Swayne to watch and learn.

'Think moody, think serious,' Luke advised, realising such an expression was second nature to Swayne. 'Shoulders straight, arms by your side. Slow, considered strides.' By now Luke had jumped off the stage and was skipping to the music while Swayne attempted to perfect his catwalk style. Luke watched carefully. He quickly realised the 'Frankenstein on roller skates' nightmare he had envisaged was far from the truth. Each time Swayne strolled down the makeshift runway, he looked more assured. He was perfectly built for the job and his expression was exquisite. Initially, Luke speculated this was to do with his deep chagrin at the entire affair. But by the end of his half-hour skip, it was clear Swayne had no problem with the required stop, stare, turn, stride.

Routine was the key to success. Each weekday at four, while their classmates charged from the school grounds at the speed of a light brigade, Luke and Swayne would quietly make their way to the school gymnasium and set about the task at hand. Jay Actenberg's bible, the portable stereo and a simple skipping rope were all they needed to further their respective bids for glory.

'What about photos?' Swayne said.

Luke took a gulp of air before replying, 'What about them?'

Swayne was striding down the catwalk, his back turned to Luke. This kind of conversation required timing and a lot of patience. When he was ready to turn and walk back towards him, face first, he replied, 'I was reading this guide last night. It says a portfolio is the most important tool at my – I mean, our disposal.'

Swayne didn't break stride or pout to address Luke. No distraction was going to keep him from performing his circuit properly.

'Don't worry about the portfolio,' Luke replied as Swayne started back down the runway. 'It's sorted.'

Everything in Luke's life of late seemed to be done in tandem with Peter Swayne. They trained in the mornings before catching the Dart and then the 46A bus to school, ate breakfast, lunch and dinner together, trained in the evenings and ended each night with a massage and each Saturday evening with a visit to the weighing scales.

Considering this flourishing symbiotic relationship, it came as no surprise to Luke when Swayne insisted on playing a part in arranging the portfolio shoot.

'Who is she, again?' Swayne asked.

'Jude, she works with me ma. You met her a couple of Saturdays back,' Luke replied. Swayne trailed behind him along Main Street in Dun Laoghaire. They approached the main entrance to the Bloomfield shopping centre. Suddenly, Luke halted. He turned to his left to survey the tinted shop front of Argos. After three weeks of hard work and sacrifice, he had shed a stone. It was time to look in a mirror. Something he had refused to do in the dark days of November.

'What's the matter?' Swayne said.

Luke concealed a smile. 'Nothing,' he said quietly, excited by the shrinking frame staring back at him in the tinted glass.

Swayne was well aware of the motive behind his sudden pause. He decided to apply some kid-glove sensitivity. 'Come on,' he said bluntly.

Teenage boys don't want a hug or a slushy 'Well done, you look fantastic' from their peers. Ignorance and cruel, obstinate gestures are the best form of flattery. Swayne played his part to perfection, shoving Luke inside the main entrance of the shopping centre. They entered Boots to find the shop floor littered with more staff than customers.

Luke walked confidently to the back of the store and a white door labelled 'PRIVATE – STAFF ONLY'. A tall, overweight security guard wearing a black, bushy moustache, grey uniform and dour expression faced them.

'All right, Luke?' he said brightly. Swayne was amazed by the instant change from frown to smile.

'What's happened to Henry, Kev – bit of a drought?' Luke replied. Swayne stood back a respectable distance while he carried on a football conversation with super-gunner Kevin. The main topic of discussion was the goal drought Thierry Henry was enduring.

'He'll come good, Kev. He'll come good,' Luke said before he and Swayne walked past into the storeroom.

'Take care,' Kevin replied. He bid them farewell with a smile and a wave before shutting the door after them. Luke and Swayne walked along a dimly lit corridor to a brown door. Luke opened the door and continued inside.

'Luke,' Martina said brightly.

Luke and Swayne had stepped inside a spacious, brightly lit office. Martina and Jude were the only people there, seated in an office cubicle at the far end of the room beside a large window and a Ballygowan water dispenser.

'What brings you two up here?' Martina said happily. She was delighted with her son's recent reversal of fortune. She knew quite well that Peter Swayne, one-time enemy, was the driving force behind the turnaround. He was now a saint in her eyes.

'Is the health store still open?' Luke said coyly.

Martina was somewhat surprised. 'Erm, no,' she said. 'Why, what's the problem?'

Luke squirmed a little. It was a paper-thin plan, but the best he could come up with on the spot. With three sets of eyes awaiting an explanation, he laid his hackneyed scheme on the line.

'Well, we wanted to make a fruit salad for dinner. But we're . . . erm, all out of fruit . . .'

Before he could finish, Martina was on her feet. 'Come on,' she said. 'Pick out what you need.' This was no good.

The main objective was to get her out of the picture, not him and Swayne.

'Why don't you surprise me?' Luke blurted out.

This remark raised the eyebrows of everyone in the office. There was something strangely fishy about a dish supposedly fruit based.

'I mean, pick out some of that exotic stuff,' Luke added.

For a moment it appeared to crash and burn, but Martina eventually smiled. 'OK. I'll be back in a few minutes. I'll leave you in the capable hands of Miss Roberts,' she said with a wry smile. 'Is that all right, Miss Roberts?' she added.

'Yes, of course, Miss Farrell,' Jude replied.

This 'Miss' business was a private joke between Martina and Jude. They giggled like schoolgirls. Obviously their boss–employee relationship was not as stern as it might have been. Luke watched his mother walk out through the brown door before turning back to Jude. She wasn't facing him. Instead her eyes were glued on Peter Swayne. Luke glanced at his trainer. The obvious attention from unfamiliar female eyes unsettled him. He bowed his head shyly.

'What's this all about?' Jude said. Luke took a seat on the table next to her. She faced him, eventually, to hear the proposition.

'I need a favour,' he said. A sudden bout of embarrassment engulfed Swayne. He turned away from the proposal and wandered out of earshot to inspect the screensaver on a distant Dell PC.

'Could you do some shots for a modelling portfolio?' Luke said quietly. Once again, Jude's attention had drifted to Swayne. The tip of her tongue loped onto her bottom lip. Drool would soon begin to dribble down her chin.

'When do you need me?' she replied breathlessly.

'Next weekend. I'm arranging locations and a wardrobe,'

Luke explained. Jude nodded vacantly. Luke turned to see what all the fuss was about. Peter Swayne had bent over a table to inspect an air purifier and his firm buttocks were on display. Luke turned away in a flash.

'Er, we'll pay for the film, paper and development,' he mumbled.

Jude was captivated. 'No need. I get free film and paper from Boots and I can use the college darkroom as much as I want.'

Luke nodded his head repeatedly. It was time to end this meeting. 'OK, great,' he said loudly, clapping his hands together. Swayne saw him get off the table. He decided to casually wander back to his side. Jude watched him stride towards her carefully.

'Listen, I'll call in sometime next week to discuss locations,' Luke said.

At that moment, Martina reappeared through the brown door with a cornucopia of island fruits and a Su Pollard style 'Hello.' Luke and Swayne turned to leave.

'Why don't you come to Baker's Corner next Thursday night? We can discuss it then,' Jude said.

Luke and Swayne turned in unison.

'It's our mid-term social. How about playing an hour-long slot as a guest DJ?' Jude continued. 'Your mum is always telling me about your great record collection.'

This idea intrigued Luke. He was always keen to show off his informed, eclectic musical taste in public. The chance to impress a group of pretentious art students was too good to turn down.

'Do you have decks?' he asked.

Jude nodded her head.

'See you Thursday,' Luke concluded with a smile. He and Swayne turned to leave. Standing in their way was a perplexed Martina holding a basket of mangos, melons and exotic fruits beginning with the letter 'm'. If she was waiting on an explanation, she would be waiting a long time. Luke smiled, took the fruit basket and walked towards the brown door. Swayne followed him, suspicious of the amorous attention his posterior might be receiving.

SHOWDOWN AT THE PALACE

Momentum is a wonderful thing when it's working your way. Luke could make it to the top of Vico Road before grinding to a gasping halt, threatening to quit and swearing at Swayne. The half-hour skip was a doddle, the swim an enjoyable challenge. As for the diet, on the completion of week four, he had lost a total of sixteen pounds. He now weighed eleven stone one, fifteen pounds short of his target. Abstaining from junk food was still hard. Loneliness was not the kind of cancer cut out with one sharp incision. Residual effects remained, tiny morsels of melancholy which still assaulted the healthy cells of optimism and determination late at night.

Peter Swayne was a diligent companion. He spent every waking moment in Luke's company. They trained together, ate together, did school work as a duo. And yet it was the words he uttered the night Luke cracked, the night his Preston North End pro contract became worthless, that inspired him to fight on through the pain. 'If you're determined to destroy all our hard work, there's nothing I can do to stop you.' It said it all really. Luke was in control of his own destiny. Not Jerome, Ella, Martina, Michael Turner. No one but himself. It summed up life in that simple, exact manner most people dismiss as cliché because they can't face up to reality and the challenge.

'You get out what you put in,' Luke said softly.

It made him smile. Even now, he could imagine these exact words coming from the mouth of Mrs Hendy in a calm, considered tone. Who would have thought she and Peter Swayne came from the same school of thought? Luke snapped out of his stoical state to check the microwave clock. Ten past ten – he had at least an hour to sift through the wardrobe unhindered. Martina was in Galway overnight for a company-sponsored course on e-commerce. D'Argo was up to his eyeballs with preparations for the charity auction at the Spring Show. He was determined to make a lasting impression in his first year as president of the Irish Cancer Trust. It was his job to co-ordinate fundraising events throughout the year. His three-pronged attack to boost the coffers had included a pro-celebrity golf tournament at the K Club in July, a five-hundred-euro-a-head Christmas dinner dance at the Berkley Court Hotel in December and, the crowning glory, a charity auction of Irish pop star memorabilia at the Spring Show in the RDS before the annual Cancer Trust fashion show.

These details had not slipped Luke's attention. In the seven months he and Martina had lived in Jonathan D'Argo's palace, the number of conversations he and his host had entered into could be counted on the fingers of a care-less crocodile-trainer. The information came from Martina and her endless stream of monologues. D'Argo didn't have time to chat with Luke. He was a busy man who could not be expected to squander precious moments on developing some semblance of a friendship with a teenage boy.

Seven months and not one question about football, not one query about his broken leg. Luke was not asking for much. Maybe the offer of a driving lesson, a part-time job in the store in Killiney village, the chance to use D'Argo's state-of-the-art fitness room in the garage when he and Swayne were facing torrential rain outside.

Nothing.

But this ongoing snub was fine with Luke. It had troubled him deeply for the three long months he was trapped inside the luxury prison. But now it was worthwhile. It provided justification for some ruthless endeavour. The kind self-made millionaires and successful businessmen thrive on. Luke would put it to D'Argo, squeeze some long overdue favours. Make him sweat a little. For far too long he had enjoyed a free lunch and an easy ride. Now it was time to settle the bill.

On the stroke of midnight, Jonathan D'Argo slipped his key inside the front door lock and ended yet another hectic day spent juggling the vast concerns of a thriving business and a glamorous charity post. Unable to muster the energy to prepare a light snack, he locked the front door behind him, set the security alarm and headed straight for bed. To his complete surprise, he found his bed a mess of clothes.

'What's going on?' he said quietly.

Luke turned to face him. This was the moment of truth. He needed to hold his nerve. 'I need to borrow some clothes,' he said casually.

D'Argo surveyed the bed. Four pure wool jumpers from esteemed designers such as Paul Smith, John Rocha and Byblos worth six hundred euros apiece were carelessly tossed in a bundle. A collection of suits, polo necks, shirts and trousers were stacked high.

'Are you collecting for a jumble sale?' he said dryly.

Luke maintained a sedate stare. He would do the decent thing and explain his actions. D'Argo would show his true colours and refuse to co-operate, forcing him to execute plan

B, or possibly C. 'I'm preparing a portfolio for a friend of mine. He wants to become a model.'

D'Argo alternated his attention between his beloved clothes and Luke. Finally he settled a stare. 'I see,' he said with a weary sigh.

Luke wasn't surprised. Inspecting the collar on one of his cherished shirts was more important to D'Argo than looking him in the eye. In reply to such a heartless brush-off, he issued a list of demands.

'I need another favour,' Luke said.

D'Argo groaned. 'Yes,' he said with obvious irritation.

'I need to get him on the runway for the Spring Show. Can you pull a few strings?'

D'Argo finished his dirt or dust inspection before turning to face Luke. It was a tiresome predicament, one that occupied his mind in the twilight moments before sleep. Of all the women to fall in love with, to *truly* fall head over heels in love with, why did he have to pick one with such cumbersome baggage?

'I take it I've little choice in the matter?' D'Argo said sardonically.

Luke didn't care for his sense of humour. 'No. You always have a choice,' he replied. 'Make an effort, don't make an effort.'

D'Argo grunted; this subsided into a smirk. This moment had been coming, it was always a matter of time. But lying down and taking punishment wasn't in the nature of the self-made millionaire. 'Well, I'm sorry, Luke. I'm sorry I don't wear luminous yellow ties and take you to some greasy chip shop each Sunday.'

Bad move. D'Argo had overstepped the mark with such a callous, unprovoked attack. Luke moved across the bedroom aggressively and stood toe-to-toe with him.

'Listen up, dickhead,' Luke snarled. 'I own you.' He stared at his foe, giving him the chance to mull over such a shocking statement in his mind. Jonathan D'Argo didn't scare easily and tutted back in derision.

'Oh, you think not?' Luke snapped. 'Well, let me spell it out for you. If it comes to a choice between me and you, who do you think she'll choose?'

D'Argo frowned. What else could he do? Luke had summed up the precarious nature of his future with Martina in a sentence. She was a mother, first and foremost. Her child came above all others.

'You don't realise how lucky you've been,' Luke explained. 'I haven't made one wave for you two. Ronald didn't get such an easy ride.'

D'Argo was most definitely on the back foot. Luke exposed his Achilles heel with the skill and precision of a seasoned pro.

'What do you want?' D'Argo said bluntly.

Luke was suitably disgusted. The trapped rat was ready to cut a deal. Ready to offer a bribe and rely on the almighty euro to get him out of trouble.

'This has got nothing to do with money . . . Jonathan,' Luke said caustically. D'Argo waited patiently to hear what it was about. Luke considered it momentarily.

'Respect,' he said crisply. Clearly an alien concept to the president of the Irish Cancer Trust.

'S-sorry?' D'Argo asked meekly.

Luke shook his head openly. 'I don't want your money or fancy gifts. All I need is for you to treat me with a shred of respect and dignity.'

D'Argo seemed confused. He had been imprisoned by a pincer-like movement. To pay some form of financial retribution was logical. But Luke let him off with the loan of the wardrobe, and a warning.

'OK, I think I understand,' D'Argo said weakly. He offered his hand for shaking.

Luke declined. 'Can you help me with the Spring Show?' he said bluntly.

D'Argo nodded. 'I'll set up a meeting with the booking agent. Just prepare a portfolio.'

Luke smiled, satisfied with his evening's work. He gathered together the clothes for the weekend shoot and marched triumphantly from the bedroom. D'Argo had been put in his place nicely. Ten minutes later, when Luke settled down to sleep, there was a knock on his bedroom door.

'What?' Luke said loudly.

D'Argo opened the door gently and smiled at Luke. 'I'm sorry, Luke . . . about everything,' he said.

Luke stared at him coldly.

'Friends?' D'Argo said mawkishly.

'Piss off,' Luke replied. He yawned, then turned over to sleep.

D'Argo was left standing red-faced in his own home by a sixteen-year-old kid from the northside of Dublin. Love and happiness had come at a high price to a man voted 'Dublin's Most Eligible Bachelor 1997'.

An Evening Spent Socialising

Thursday was a red-letter day in the calendar for Luke and Swayne. The Dun Laoghaire Art College mid-term social was a chance to let their hair down, after four and a half weeks of strenuous physical exercise, healthy eating and nightly massages. The chance to engage in any activity that didn't involve adhering to a predetermined schedule was a liberating prospect for Luke.

Swayne, however, seemed somewhat reluctant to throw himself into the spirit of things. 'You can't go drinking,' he said bluntly.

Luke stopped searching in his wardrobe and turned to face him. 'Give me a break. This is supposed to be a fun night out,' he insisted.

Swayne folded his arms. He had no intention of allowing Luke to indulge in 'a fun night out' if it meant jeopardising weeks of hard work. 'No alcohol, no junk food,' he said.

Luke protested falsetto, 'What?'

Swayne stared back with a worrying sense of conviction. Agreement on this stipulation seemed to be crucial if they were to attend the social that evening. Luke groaned in dismay. 'OK, OK, no alcohol, no junk food.'

Swayne nodded his head. Luke tutted derisively and went back to his wardrobe to find something to wear. He made a snide comment. 'Jesus, you really know how to suck the enjoyment out of things.'

Swayne didn't reply.

'I bet there's state-of-the-art cyborgs somewhere in the world who party more than we do.'

Luke pulled out a smart black polo-neck jumper. He turned to lay it on the bed. Peter Swayne was staring at a picture frame hanging on the wall above Luke's headboard. The photo was of the victorious Stretford Enders celebrating the All-Ireland Cup Final win against Stella Maris. Luke coughed politely. Swayne glanced back at him momentarily.

'Was he really that good?' he asked softly. Luke noticed the sadness in Swayne's eyes. It took a moment to reply.

'Yeah. He was great.'

Swayne spun round from the photo slowly. His head was bowed. 'I didn't go to watch him,' he said quietly, unable to look Luke in the eye. 'I wasn't busy that Sunday. I just didn't bother.'

Silence filled the room like water rushing through the breached hull of a sinking ship. Tongue-tied by the revelation and the re-emergence of guilt, Luke could find no words of comfort or consolation. Swayne took this reticence as a damnation of his actions. He sped from the bedroom. 'I'll wait in the kitchen,' he mumbled on the way.

Luke wanted to call him back, to confess his own tainted acts of abandonment, but he had no time to wallow in the mire of self-loathing. Three months in that pit was enough to last a lifetime. There was a train to catch, a bus to board, a social to attend. A life to live.

Jude stood outside Baker's Corner pub awaiting the arrival of Luke and Swayne at the 46A bus stop across the road. It never crossed her mind they would catch the 75 and their appearance on her blind side caused her to jump. 'Jesus,' she gasped. 'You scared me half to death.'

Jude had made a real effort for the evening. She dispensed with her casual, easy-going, some might say scruffy attitude towards clothing, ditching faded flares and a threadbare top for a tight, white Kookai T-shirt and a pair of black hipsters that accentuated her shapely figure. Foundation, lipstick and blush procured from the storeroom in Boots liberated her striking good looks.

'Sorry we're late,' Luke said. A heavy navy record bag was draped over his shoulder. It was Swayne who bore the main brunt of Jay's enormous record collection. He carried a huge cardboard box stuffed full of rare, mint-condition vinyl.

'Hello,' Jude said to Swayne, making a special effort to include him in the conversation. Swayne nodded his head shyly.

'Do you need a hand with that?' she asked, inventing any excuse to size up his bulging biceps.

'Erm, no thanks,' Swayne replied softly.

'Right, then. Let's go inside,' she said brightly. The trio entered the side entrance of the pub and climbed the staircase to the main function room on the first floor. Jude introduced Luke to her friend Sadie, a tall, thin girl with a striking head of red hair as thick as a lion's mane. She was studying radio broadcasting at the art college and was also in charge of music for the evening.

'Are all these yours?' Sadie said in amazement. She handled a copy of the Sex Pistols' *Never Mind the Bollocks* with reverent care.

'Me da's,' Luke replied.

'Er, Peter, would you like a drink?' Jude said politely.

Luke glanced upward. Swayne was clearly unnerved by Jude's attention. He shrugged his shoulders indecisively. This behaviour could easily be misconstrued as rude, but Luke was becoming accustomed to Peter Swayne's slight quirks. This was nerves.

'Yeah. He'll have a pint of Carlsberg. I'll have a mineral water,' Luke said confidently. He gave her a look of assurance. The signal travelled silently from one brain to the other: 'Don't take offence. He's just shy.'

Jude smiled. Message received loud and clear. When she walked off to the bar, Swayne shuffled to Luke's side and tried to whisper a disapproving comment in his ear.

'Don't start,' Luke said sharply, cutting him off at the pass. 'She's a lovely girl who is just trying to be friendly.' He couldn't resist voicing a sly dig that had come to mind: 'I know, I know. You're not used to warm women.'

Luke smirked. To stab a full stop at the end of his quip he needed to walk away from the DJ box. The only logical place to go was the bar. Swayne sighed.

'Ha, ha, ha,' he said sarcastically.

The one and only positive aspect of alcohol consumption is the removal of inhibition. When taken in the right quantities, alcohol unlocks the insecurities of shy, bashful folk, affording them the opportunity to interact socially in situations they would normally run a mile from. By the end of Luke's hour-long set, Swayne and Jude were standing at the bar, laughing and joking. It brought a smile to his face. They made a nice couple. Over the course of five weeks, his opinion of Peter Swayne as a human being had been altered beyond recognition. Beforehand, his fate as Cecilia's lifetime lapdog would have brought a fiendish smile to his face. Now, he found himself rooting for Swayne and Jude to live happily ever after.

'Great set, man,' a voice said. In front of Luke stood a rake-thin radio broadcasting student with brush-like brown hair and big brown eyes who looked no more than twelve. He was wearing an aqua-marine Charlatans T-shirt and a pair of brown cords.

'Me name's Eoin,' the kid said. He had a thick culchie accent.

Luke stuck out his hand. 'Luke, pleased to meet you,' he replied.

'How did you know to play "Can't Get Used to Losing You" after "You Don't Know What It's Like"?' he asked happily as he presented Luke with a bottle of orange Bacardi Breezer.

Luke declined. 'I'm on the water,' he explained.

Out of the corner of his eye, Luke noticed Swayne and Jude heading for the exit. It was an encouraging sign, one that brought a warm feeling to his heart. He decided to allow them the privacy they deserved. 'Do you fancy a drink, Eoin?' Luke said.

The next two hours were taken care of by this one simple gesture. Luke enjoyed a great night. Entertained and lauded by Sadie, Eoin and the rest of the radio broadcasting class, his only misfortune was his alcohol abstinence. The number of people offering to buy him a drink snaked into double figures by the time last orders rolled around. There was still no sign of Swayne and Jude, who were most probably up to no good outside. Let them have their fun, Luke thought to himself. He turned back to Eoin and his bespectacled buddy Bren, who was a fellow northsider and bore an uncanny resemblance to John Lennon. The conversation was currently centred on the majesty of The Clash over The Jam. Luke was fighting Weller's corner.

'Let me put it this way. Five number ones in five years. *And* I'm talking 'seventy-seven to 'eighty-two. A lot harder to get a number one single back then.'

The sight of Swayne striding across the dance floor with purpose surprised Luke no end. Jude didn't appear for a further fifteen seconds, and when she did emerge from the shadows, she wasn't smiling.

'I have to go,' Swayne said abruptly. Luke looked up at him. Something had gone wrong. He got up from the table and ushered Swayne away from the radio broadcasting crew.

'What's the matter?' Luke said discreetly.

Swayne tried to speak, but couldn't explain. It was something difficult to divulge in a packed function room. Luke tried to help him along, but before he could speak Swayne pulled a ten-euro note from the back pocket of his jeans. 'Listen, I'll see you in the morning. Get a taxi home with the gear.'

Luke was completely dumbfounded. He watched Peter Swayne turn and bolt towards the fire escape like a stampeding buffalo. Whatever had happened outside the pub that night was so severe, he couldn't face walking past Jude. At that moment a sudden flashback hit Luke like a cannonball. Last July in the Vortex disco in Liverpool: David Swayne made a carbon-copy escape from the attentions of a stunning blonde Luke tried to pair him off with. It was a creepy coincidence. He made an immediate bee-line for Jude, who stood at the bar waiting to be served. Initially, he suspected inappropriate behaviour from Swayne had landed him a sturdy slap to the face. But his transformation from shy, bumbling bag of nerves to sex-starved monster seemed unlikely.

'What happened?' Luke asked bluntly.

Jude sighed sadly. 'I don't know, Luke. I don't know.'

PORTFOLIO SHOOT

Swàyne refused to talk about it all day Friday. At first Luke
was determined to find out what had gone wrong, but as the
day progressed he could sense his companion's need for space
and time. The one thing Luke hated more than anything in
the world was a barrage of questions when he wasn't in the
humour for talking. Respecting someone's privacy is
important. Especially if you value your own so highly.

On Saturday morning Jude arrived at D'Argo's palace
promptly at ten a.m. Luke and Swayne had been jogging
earlier, but were now showered and freshly changed for her
arrival. The tension was surprisingly bearable. Luke stood
back, looking after the costumes, while Jude instructed
Swayne to adopt various poses. Weather-wise, March
presented them with an unusually mild and pleasant day.
The first location was D'Argo's back garden. Then they
moved to Killiney beach. Then it was a quick train ride
north to Blackrock, where they took full advantage of the
wonderful locations in the public park. Back once more to
Dun Laoghaire harbour, and the last port of call was Dalkey
quarry. Five separate locations, fourteen costume changes
and ten rolls of film later, the whole affair was wrapped up
by half five that evening.

'I'll give you a call on Tuesday. You can look at the contact
sheets with me,' Jude said quietly.

'Yeah, thanks,' Luke replied.

Jude walked from D'Argo's front porch without saying a word to Swayne. He returned the compliment. It didn't seem to be an angry silence. Whatever had happened on Thursday evening seemed more to do with unfortunate than with offensive. When Jude disappeared from view, Luke turned on Swayne.

'Follow me,' he said firmly.

'Where?' Swayne replied.

'Just follow me.' Luke marched down the driveway, skipping rope in hand. He would get to the bottom of this mess if it took him all evening.

Dalkey quarry and the Air Safety beacon were a short walk from D'Argo's palace. Luke stood face-to-face with Swayne on the concrete slabs that surrounded the towering pole and bluntly demanded an explanation. 'What happened?' he said.

Swayne stared at him sadly. It was something he found difficult to talk about, that much was clear. Luke decided to employ some pep-talk style coaxing. 'Look, I'm not being nosy. I just want to know what went wrong,' he said honestly.

Swayne stared at the ground a while before eventually looking up at Luke. He repeated this cycle four times. Each revolution brought him a little closer to spilling the beans. Luke began to skip, illustrating the 'take your time' addendum nicely. Swayne turned away from him to start.

'We were outside the pub, about to kiss . . .' He stalled inexplicably.

'Yeah,' Luke said, prompting helpfully.

'But I couldn't do it.'

Luke waited for Swayne to turn round and face him before he asked the obvious question. 'Why not?' he said.

This was the clincher. Swayne opened his mouth to reveal the classified information, the missing X-file that had kept Luke awake, speculating, till the early hours on Friday morning.

'Because I've never been with anyone but Cecilia,' he said unhappily.

Luke stopped skipping. It was the worst reaction possible, but he just couldn't help himself. Peter Swayne, a one-woman man. Impressive? No. Unbelievable? *Yes*. The fact that he could stay faithful to one girl was both commendable and quite remarkable. But why he would stay faithful to Cecilia Giles was baffling. This was the girl who asked out another bloke at his brother's funeral. The girl who left him standing alone on Grafton Street in the pouring rain while she partied the night away with some midget guinea photographer.

What a waste of devotion.

'So, what are you saying? You don't fancy Jude?' Luke said, shamelessly changing the subject.

Swayne stared out to sea. 'No. I *do*,' he said sincerely. 'But what's the point in me learning to be a model if we don't go through with this plan?'

This was Luke's opportunity to convince Swayne his life would be unadulterated bliss without Cecilia. He could massage that bruised ego, emphasise the many virtues that had grown and flourished since the pouting blonde witch ejected him from her life.

But he couldn't do it. 'Yeah. I suppose you have a point,' Luke said softly.

In a split second of contemplation he came to the conclusion that advising people about matters of the heart was an exercise in futility. It was a counterpoint to Swayne's comments about the curry – destroying all their hard work.

No matter how skilfully and subtly he manipulated the mind to seek pastures new, those visceral feelings of love would manifest themselves in some way, shape or form.

'Do what your gut tells you to do,' Luke said. He began to skip, realising they were falling behind schedule.

Peter Swayne stared at the cracks in the concrete slabs thoughtfully. Jude had caused a conflict in his mind. Where before there was nothing but Cecilia, now a new entity had annexed a piece of his heart.

STAGES TWO AND THREE

Luke took care of things single-handedly after the weekend photo shoot. He met Jude in the art college darkroom to look through contact sheets. They debated which negatives to print for the portfolio. The topic of discussion was unavoidable, but Jude cleared it up before it became an awkward stumbling block.

'I saw a picture of this Cecilia person,' she said quietly.

Luke lifted the magnifying glass from his left eye. 'She's a bitch,' he replied confidently.

Jude stared into space. Luke's attempt to soften the blow had little effect.

'She's beautiful,' Jude confessed sadly.

The rest of the afternoon's work was conducted in near silence. Luke waited patiently for a second opportunity to encourage the development of a Jude–Swayne axis, but his input wasn't necessary or helpful. At half six that evening he waved goodbye to her at the 75 bus stop, a thick folder of high-quality prints tucked safely beneath his arm. Swayne was stationed on Killiney beach at half seven, waiting to swim. When Luke arrived the temptation was to have a quiet word on Jude's behalf. But in the end, he decided to keep his nose out of other people's private affairs. Intrusion was a tricky business.

* * *

'Hop on,' Swayne said.

Luke obeyed this order enthusiastically. The Easiscale gave good news.

'Three pounds,' Swayne said brightly.

'Yes,' Luke replied happily. He jumped off the scales and danced about his bedroom in delight.

Swayne jotted down the results in his small green notebook. 'Ten stone, ten pounds. That's a stone and a half lost,' he said proudly.

Luke glanced in the mirror of his Sliderobe. The old Luke Farrell was emerging from the flabby figure with the constant frown who had sublet his life for three months. The old smile was back.

'Towel, bed,' Swayne said. Luke jumped to attention like a well-drilled army private. The routine was second nature. He assumed the correct position on his bed and let Swayne's hands do the rest.

'I've got a meeting tomorrow with the booking agent for the Spring Show,' Luke said. Swayne didn't reply. He continued the massage. 'I have to go in to Grafton Street, but I'll be back for the swim in the evening,' Luke added.

Again, no reply. Swayne completed his work and offered a curt 'See you in the morning' before disappearing out the front door. Luke was accustomed to short and sweet discussions with Swayne, but somehow he sensed a subdued spirit sagging out of the front door that evening. Perhaps the Jude affair had affected him more than he was prepared to admit.

Saturday was a momentous day. Not only did Luke manage to complete the five-mile course without stalling once; he also completed stage three of his plan and secured Peter Swayne a spot on the catwalk for the Spring Show. Maurice

Bates, the managing director of Image Inc. modelling agency, was more than impressed with Swayne's portfolio. However, the key factor in his decision to hire a virtual unknown with no previous catwalk experience was a phone call days earlier from his close friend and regular four-ball partner Jonathan D'Argo, who highly recommended the hiring of young Swayne. It was a done deal before Luke walked into the offices of Image Inc. Connections count in Dublin.

With a firm handshake and a pleasant smile, Luke left Image Inc. and headed for Fleet Street to catch a 46A. He wanted to stop off at Merrion Grove to announce the wonderful news to Swayne before the evening's swim. It was five to six when he reached the front door. He pressed the doorbell once and waited patiently for an answer. Jack Swayne appeared moments later.

'Luke,' he said in surprise.

'Hello, Mr Swayne,' Luke faltered in reply. 'Is Peter there?'

The empty look in Jack Swayne's eyes resembled a hideous scar. The pain of David's death was still clearly visible. In November the church had been packed to the rafters and awash with genuine tears of sorrow, but those tears had long since evaporated under the unstoppable march of time. The tears welling within Jack Swayne's eyes were as fresh as those cried five months earlier.

'No, Luke. He popped out to the newsagent's a while back,' he said vacantly.

Luke made his excuses and walked from the front garden. A quick glance back at Jack Swayne pulling shut the porch door triggered that putrid feeling of guilt in his stomach. He grimaced and shivered, unable to contain that dreaded cold sweat creeping up his spine. Upon his exit from Merrion Park estate, he turned left to check out Morley's newsagent's on the slip road off the dual carriageway. It was the sight in the periphery of his vision that offered up the clue which had been staring him in the face for twenty-odd hours now. Deansgrange cemetery.

David Swayne was born on 21 March 1986. If he were still alive he would be celebrating his sixteenth birthday. Luke entered the cemetery from the side gate adjacent to the dual carriageway and made his way slowly between a long row of headstones. Peter Swayne's sedate mood over the last two days was suddenly understandable. While the community at large would for ever recognise David's anniversary in November, family and close friends had the pain of an obsolete birthday to deal with. Daylight was almost gone when Luke sighted Peter Swayne, standing next to the grave. He turned his head slightly at the sound of footsteps crunching the gravel path behind him. Luke and Swayne stared at one another in silence for a good half minute.

'Sixteen,' Swayne said, turning his head back to the grave.

'Yeah,' Luke replied quietly.

'I've been thinking a lot about last summer,' Swayne said softly. 'I mean, how come I didn't find it strange? Someone who lived for football suddenly deciding to quit.' He turned back to Luke. 'I knew something was wrong. After Everton knocked him back. I knew he needed help.'

Swayne stopped and stared intensely into space. His face turned red with anger and self-loathing as tears began streaming down his cheeks. These were emotions and states of mind Luke was all to familiar with.

'But do you think I ever once knocked on his bedroom door and asked, "Are you OK?"'

Luke couldn't offer an answer.

'I was his big brother. I was supposed to look after him,

protect him. But all I ever gave him was a hard time,' Swayne sobbed on.

Luke hesitated on his next move. He could offer an arm round the shoulder, a squeeze of comfort, words of kindness. The only problem being, these frank confessions of neglect were spot on. Swayne had treated David poorly in public. What private moments of brotherly love and affection he displayed were open to speculation.

Luke was on the verge of saying something when Swayne resumed his speech.

'We went to a family barbecue at my Uncle Ken's house last August. He lives near you, on Dalkey Avenue. I brought Cecilia and Casey along. David brought no one. All that night he was standing on his own – he wouldn't talk to anyone, not even Les. Then around twelve o'clock I saw him swipe a nagon of vodka from the kitchen. He walked into the back garden and disappeared over the wall.'

Swayne had to stop a while. The pain was overwhelming. Luke wanted to intervene, but before he had made a definitive decision the story started up again.

'I found him two hours later. Legless on the back lawn. But I never said a word to him. I just ignored it. The most blatant, obvious cry for help anyone could ever make and I ignored it.'

Swayne was shouting at this point. He dropped to his knees by the headstone and bowed his head in a listless sob. Luke watched with a strange sensation of guilt and salvation. His own feelings of neglect had been tempered by this confession. But complete acquittal proved elusive. It was just another example of the imperfections in life. No one could claim outright responsibility for David's demise. As with all accidents and tragedies, it was an intricate combination of people, places, actions and non-actions that brought about the awful conclusion. There was one terrible truth. Peter Swayne's confession brought peace to Luke's soul. He could now accept his part in the tragedy and get on with things.

'It's not your fault, Peter,' Luke said softly. He squatted low to Swayne's left, placing a hand on his shoulder as an act of compassion. 'We all played a part in it. Me, Tonka, the lads, Jerome. Whatever he needed to hear, none of us said it.'

Swayne cut in. 'But I was his brother,' he hissed angrily.

'. . . And I was his friend,' Luke interrupted. 'And we both let him down. But it wasn't our fault. We didn't want him to commit suicide. We just wanted him to be happy.'

Swayne looked at Luke, tears running down his cheek. 'I hate myself,' he sobbed.

It was an emotional moment. Luke thought about it for a second while Swayne cried his eyes out. He decided it was a worthwhile gambit. Comedy was the only remedy at hand.

'I hate you too,' he said with a smile. 'You're one class-A arsehole, and you get on my tits something rotten.'

There was a brief impasse when it all seemed to have backfired. But Luke kept smiling, forcing his former foe to turn it round, to let go of the self-loathing. Eventually, he did so. Swayne began to laugh, allowing his grief to build into a rollicking roar. Luke followed suit. Together in the darkness they coughed in hysterics. The pain and bitterness evaporated overhead in a noxious cloud of laughter and tears.

SWALLOWING PRIDE

Life is full of coincidence. Swayne's debut on the catwalk at the RDS Spring Show took place the same weekend the scouts from Spurs, Newcastle Utd, Man City and Aston Villa promised to return to check on the progress of Luke and his repaired right leg. On the Tuesday evening beforehand he walked up Woodlawn Drive to rejoin his one-time team-mates for a training session. In the period of time between January and April the Stretford Enders had slumped to four straight defeats and three frustrating draws. What for a long time looked like a canter to the Division B league title had now become a tense two-horse race between themselves and Valley Rangers, who held a two-point advantage.

'All right?' Luke said to Jerome.

His sudden arrival was no surprise. The manager of the Enders had been keeping in close contact with Martina, who acted as his mole. Once he learned of the successful regime of diet and training he set about preparing the path for Luke's return to the fold. However, the other players had not been kept abreast of developments.

'What's he doing here?' Nally said rudely.

Luke bowed his head shamefaced.

'Nally, shut it,' Jerome ordered.

Luke had a fair idea he would cop such forthright criticism upon his return. To pre-empt such bitter comments he decided to apologise publicly.

'Erm, I know what you're all thinking. I've only come back because the scouts are coming to watch us play this weekend—'

'What's all this "us" crap?' Nally interrupted.

'Nally, I said shut your trap,' Jerome replied.

Luke noticed the tension and anxiety in every face. They formed an unruly mob alongside Jerome. His dramatic return was sure to split the team into two camps. For and against.

'I know what you're all thinking, but it's not true. I just want to be an Ender again,' Luke said sincerely.

Nally tutted in derision. Luke glanced his way, realising five or six players shared his opinion. Copper, Ille, Lofty and Leslie – the old guard would support his position. But Tosh Pollock, Nally and the other new boys had no memory of the good old days. All they recalled was their uphill slog through the current season without the help of Captain Fantastic, who had sulked off home in mid-January.

'Right. Listen up. This kid has given more to this team than any other player standing here,' Jerome said proudly. 'If anyone doesn't agree with me, speak up now.'

No one said a word. Nally and his crew kicked their boots into the muddy ground scornfully. It was a contentious issue. One that could not be resolved in a matter of minutes. A longer period of time was required to heal the wound. This was not a cut or bruise. It was a deep incision.

'OK, six laps of the park. Go,' Jerome said loudly.

Luke ran with the back markers. Along the way Copper Martin smiled and patted his shoulder. Ille gave him a thumbs up and Lofty whispered, 'Welcome back, Skip.' Nally and Pollock glanced at him in disdain. But as Mrs

Hendy would often say, 'If someone loves you for you, someone hates you for the same reason.'

Training was a doddle. After eight weeks of intense preparation Luke had not only lost a scratch under two stone, he had also built up his stamina to a higher level than before the injury. He was raring to go for Saturday. At the end of the session, Jerome offered his prodigal son a lift home to D'Argo's palace.

'I heard about Michael Turner and Preston,' Jerome said quietly.

'Yeah, well. That's life,' Luke replied stoically.

Jerome nodded. 'I'm sure he passed on your file to Evans and Rush, but I haven't heard any word from them.'

Luke glanced at Jerome in surprise. When he had refused the manager's offer of help in late January he had assumed Project Luke Farrell had been consigned to the dustbin. After all, with Luke having severed his link with Ella and then the Stretford Enders, what duty did Jerome have to look after his best interests?

'When your mum told me about you and Peter I decided to leave you to it,' Jerome said. He turned to Luke with a sombre expression. 'I thought you might move on to Home Farm or Stella Maris.'

'Why would I do that?' Luke replied.

Jerome concentrated on the road a while. He shrugged his shoulders, recognising Luke's faithful stare in anticipation of an answer. 'I don't know,' he said. 'I suppose I thought you were making a fresh start, moving on.'

Luke didn't know what to say. It was a delicate situation. The revival of his fledgling career would for ever be down to the intervention of Peter Swayne, not Jerome Barnes. If everything worked out and he managed to forge a career as a professional footballer, he would have to name his former nemesis as his unlikely saviour.

'I just want to play football,' Luke said cryptically.

Jerome smiled. He was happy to go along with the subterfuge.

THE ΠIGHT BEFORE

There was no let-up in the training schedule on Swayne's part. On Friday evening he commandeered the school gymnasium so that he could perform a dress rehearsal of his nine costume changes at the Spring Show to music while Luke skipped out front. In the space of thirty minutes both he and Swayne displayed the fruits of eight weeks' hard labour. The smooth, confident stride down the makeshift catwalk. The diffident facial expression. Best of all was his clean and crisp stop, pose, turn, retreat.

Peter Swayne was *smoking*.

Luke skipped at a frenetic pace. At the same time he carried on a conversation with his trainer about the party politics that had split the Stretford Enders in two like a meat cleaver cutting through a watermelon. When the stopwatch lying atop of Swayne's schoolbag beep-beeped to signal the end of the half-hour workout, he still had a couple of costume changes to go through. Luke took a seat and slugged back a bottle of Lucozade Sport. It was the perfect opportunity to brief Swayne on the final phase of his plan.

'By the way, when Cecilia catches a glimpse of you tomorrow, there's a certain way you need to behave to make the most of her interest.'

Swayne walked to the end of the catwalk and struck a pose. 'Go on,' he said, without looking Luke's way.

'The key word is aloofness,' Luke shouted as Swayne

retreated back down the stage. 'When she finds out you're a model she'll be a jumble of questions. What, why, when, how, all that crap. If you're to make the most of this situation, you have to – I repeat, *have* to – be too busy to talk with her there and then.'

Swayne was changing into his final costume of the dress rehearsal. 'I just ignore her?' he said doubtfully.

'*Yes!*' Luke exclaimed passionately. 'You brush her off big style.'

'The Bends' by Radiohead started blaring out of the stereo speakers. The music compiled on the cassette tape matched the exact running order for the Spring Show as specified in the information pack sent to Peter Swayne along with his one-off contract and security passes. He made his final stride down the catwalk.

'Why do I ignore her?' he asked.

Luke took a running leap and propelled himself up onto the catwalk. He followed Swayne back down the runway ranting and raving like a preacher.

'Because you've never ignored her before. Ever! She hasn't seen you in two months and as far as she's concerned you're sitting at home each night crying yourself to sleep over her.'

Luke manoeuvred himself in front of Swayne. 'But when she sees you tomorrow her jaw will hit the fucking floor. Not only are you out and about; you're making a career for yourself. When you see her, you smile, say, "Hi, how are you? Sorry, can't talk. Places to go, people to meet." And BOOM! You walk off. Remember those four little words: putty in your hands.'

Swayne smiled. Luke replied in kind. They packed up the costumes, stereo and skipping rope and left for D'Argo's palace. The weather had been improving steadily all that week. It was shaping up for a lovely, long spring evening. The perfect setting for a swim.

The grounds of Woodlawn Comprehensive were empty when Swayne and Luke stepped into the evening sunlight. They walked up the driveway and prepared to cross Woodlawn Drive and cut through the park to reach the 46A bus stop. That is, until they spotted a group of kids. Luke recognised the scene instantly. Eight weeks earlier he had seen the same gang taunt their chubby victim and extort his lunch money. Back then Luke was so badly mired in the pit of self-pity he was powerless to intervene. That restriction no longer applied.

Swayne watched in confusion as Luke sprinted across Woodlawn Drive. He headed straight for the ringleader, a blond bag of wind who held the chubby kid by the scruff of his shirt collar.

'Get your hands off him,' Luke ordered fiercely. The gang scattered in fear. Luke proceeded to break blondie's choke hold and shove him forcefully. The surprise nature of the attack paralysed the junior thug with shock. He stumbled backwards and fell to the ground.

Luke kneeled down and applied an identical choke hold to the one blondie had employed moments earlier on the chubby kid.

'If you ever lay a finger on him or any other kid in that school again, I'll break you in two,' he said with an snarl.

Blondie wasn't about to argue out the point. He nodded his head in terror until Luke released the choke hold and allowed him to flee.

Luke issued a loud proclamation to the other gang members, who held position forty yards away at the goalposts. 'That goes for you lot, too.'

Whatever words of clandestine defiance were uttered out of earshot mattered little. Luke was a respected figurehead in the student community of Woodlawn Comprehensive. To start a war with someone of his stature was a bad move. He stared at the scattered gang members a little longer before turning to address the chubby kid. He was standing in awe of his unlikely saviour, who smiled at him and offered his hand.

'I'm Luke,' he said.

'Erm, I'm Danny,' the kid replied nervously.

Luke reached into his schoolbag and pulled a page from a science copy book. 'Have you got a pen, Danny?' he said.

Danny searched his schoolbag frantically and produced a red Bic biro. He handed it to Luke, who scribbled down his phone number on the piece of paper.

'Danny, if you want to do some fitness training give me a ring,' Luke said awkwardly. He looked Danny in the eye. 'But, you know. If you just want a chat, give me a ring,' he added kindly.

Such a random act of kindness and sincerity was hard to believe. Danny sensed an elaborate practical joke in the offing. Luke understood the root of his paranoia. Convincing the kid that his intentions were honourable would be difficult. That is, until Swayne stepped in to sweeten the deal.

'I'll tell you what, Danny. We'll meet you at the bike shed Monday lunch time. Let those little gimps see whose friend they're messing with.'

Danny smiled. He nodded his head. 'OK, I'll see you then.'

Luke and Swayne watched Danny walk from Woodlawn Park with his head held high. That wretched feeling of loneliness had been dispelled for the time being. He doubted whether Luke or Swayne would turn up on Monday, but he

DAY OF DESTINY

Saturday morning without the sound of a six-thirty alarm bell followed by a five-mile jog round Killiney Head seemed strangely barren to Luke. His body clock was unaware of the change in schedule and set the wheels of consciousness in motion as per usual. He sat on his bed listening to the waves caress the shore below. After weighing in the night before at ten stone one he had developed a strong fixation with remaining naked. Staring at his physique restored to its finest in the full-length Sliderobe mirror brought a warm sense of pride and achievement. He had earned these trim curves and would never take them for granted again. Saturday 10 April was a red-letter day for all concerned in the household. The Spring Show was a priceless opportunity for Jonathan D'Argo to write his name in the sky for the upper crust of Irish society to see. He rushed around like a headless chicken all morning mumbling things to himself. Luke ate a bowl of cornflakes and watched with a refined sense of indifference.

'Luke, do you need a lift?' Martina said. She was standing in front of the hall mirror fixing her hair with an afro comb.

He decided to spare her the added hassle. 'Na. I'll bus it,' he replied.

'Oh yes, Luke,' D'Argo said deliberately, on his reappearance in the kitchen. 'I managed to get you an access-all-areas pass.'

Luke didn't reciprocate the cheesy smile. Instead he stood

up from the kitchen counter and washed out his bowl at the sink before announcing, 'Snap.'

D'Argo stared at the identical marble-green pass provided by Image Inc. modelling agency for Luke as a recognised talent agent. It was a beautiful coup.

'Oh, I see,' D'Argo mumbled quietly as Luke walked off, victorious. After six months of outright neglect, any sincere or half-arsed attempt at bridge-building would receive Loch Ness monster style scepticism. D'Argo had a lesson to learn. Trust and respect are earned, not bought.

Swayne was waiting at the school gates when Luke arrived at half nine. He wore a simple black Adidas tracksuit and sipped a bottle of Ballygowan mineral water.

'You're back and all?' Luke said in surprise.

'Yeah, Dad gave me a lift,' he replied. 'All we have to do is be there for make-up at half two.'

Luke and Swayne walked into the car park in unison. The opposition team bus was parked next to the bike shed. St Paul's were sitting in fourth place in Division B and had trounced the Enders five–one in the league two months earlier. Over by the dressing rooms, Nally, Tosh Pollock and their crew stood in a small circle while Copper Martin and the old guard sat next to the basketball court. When Luke approached with Swayne, Copper, who had taken the mantle of acting team captain in his absence, called a team meeting.

'Lads, gather round,' he said loudly.

Swayne stepped back and allowed the huddle to take place in private. Luke stood next to the Burke brothers and listened to the address of the stand-in captain.

'We can't afford any arguments today. This game is too important,' Copper said frankly. Nally and Tosh conceded the point. There was still a league championship to play for. That fact took precedent over any internal finger-pointing. 'I call a truce.'

Copper looked at the faces directly involved and demanded recognition. Nally didn't fancy being first to conform but Luke saved his blushes by offering his hand. Nally and his faction were gracious enough to accept the truce. The meeting ended with a Copper Martin led battle cry. Before joining the Enders in the home dressing room, Luke caught a glimpse of four vaguely familiar faces locked in discussion by a corner flag. The same faces that had watched from the sideline six months earlier had returned to witness his comeback. Luke turned to Swayne and offered a thumbs-up before jogging to the dressing room to ready himself for battle. He had ninety minutes to rekindle his career.

Jerome entered the dressing room to find the lads in varying states of undress. Some had socks, shorts, boots and shin pads on while some were still in jeans and jumpers. Luke had been eager to ready himself for action and stripped before anyone else. He sat beside Copper awaiting his customary number nine jersey.

'All right, listen up,' Jerome said loudly. The boys turned their eyes to the manager as he read out the team from a white sheet clamped to a red clipboard.

'Alan in goal. Muffin, Edgar, Nally, Éclair, back four. Lofty, Copper, Tosh, Leslie, Ille in midfield. Con up front.'

Luke stared at Jerome, sure he had made a mistake. The named players moved to the kit bag lying on the treatment table in the centre of the room and took out the jerseys numbered one to eleven. Luke had been left on the bench. He sat still for a moment, trying to interpret such a giant bombshell in rational terms. He tried to look on it as a credible tactical decision to benefit both himself and the Enders. Jerome stood beside the dressing-room door with Daniel Popsecu. They studied the team-sheet together and whispered comments in each other's ears. The first eleven were now kitted out. Nally and Tosh threw several smug glances in Luke's direction.

'Luke,' Copper said quietly.

Luke focused on his captain, who handed him the number fourteen jersey. 'Thanks,' he replied vacantly.

Jerome clapped his hands to call his team to order. 'OK, lads. From the first whistle,' he said proudly.

Nally started the chanting and soon the dressing room was in uproar. Copper led his team out to the tune of a charged cacophony. It was an intimidating sound for the opposition to hear across the hall. It would have been louder, but one member of the Enders squad decided not to join in with his team-mates.

'Luke,' Jerome said in surprise. 'What's going on?'

The manager was standing outside the dressing-room door watching Luke remove his boots, shin pads, shorts and socks. Luke regarded him bitterly, taunting the mock shock in his expression and tone of voice.

'I'm going home,' he said bluntly.

'You're what?' Jerome replied. 'Why?' He stepped inside the dressing room and shut the door behind him.

Luke stared his way with a bittersweet smile. 'I have to hand it to you. You'll go to some lengths to get your own back.'

'What are you talking about?' Jerome replied sharply.

Luke stuffed his kit back into his sports bag. 'I never thought you'd be so petty.'

'What?' Jerome replied.

'Ruining my big chance just so you can get back at me for walking out on your stupid team.'

Jerome was stunned. He watched Luke get back into his civilian attire, unable to comment on the accusation slung in his face moments earlier. When he was ready to leave, Luke took a hold of the number fourteen jersey and flung it at Jerome's chest.

'Thanks for nothing,' he said. He walked towards the door.

'You can't leave, Luke,' Jerome said.

'Watch me,' Luke replied without breaking stride.

Swayne had turned his attention on the entrance to the dressing rooms after the Enders trotted out onto the pitch. He quickly noticed the absence of Luke in the squad listed one to eleven. It meant a place on the subs bench and a possible temper tantrum.

'Luke,' Jerome said loudly.

Swayne watched Luke burst through the door like a bullet from a gun. Jerome shouted his name again. He rushed out of the door after him. He stopped Luke by grabbing his arm and proceeded to talk. It was an explanation of some sort but it cut no ice with Luke. He shook off his manager not once but twice and continued to steam out of Woodlawn Comprehensive.

'Luke,' Jerome called once more. His skills of persuasion had been tested beyond their limit. If the morning were not to end in disaster Peter Swayne would have to intervene. It required a fifty-yard sprint to catch and overtake Luke.

'What's the story?' Swayne said.

Luke tried to manoeuvre past his trainer, so strong was his determination to illustrate his pride to team-mates, scouts and the public at large.

'Luke,' Swayne said, applying his hands to his shoulders. This was a move that broke the steely-eyed emotion for a brief second. Luke stared at him with a sense of anger tainted with sadness. Every time he made a rash decision nowadays he had to explain it in minute detail.

'Look, I'm not in the humour, just let me go,' Luke snapped.

'No. Tell me what happened,' Swayne replied bravely.

Luke sighed. Yet again self-determination and the power to execute reckless acts had been scuppered by the interference of a foreign body. Swayne was something much stronger than a parental force. He was a compass of common sense and logic that kept volatile emotions in check.

'Don't you watch *Star Trek*?' Luke said angrily. 'Ever heard of a little thing called the prime directive?'

Swayne ignored the reference. He didn't care for science fiction and realised that Luke was attempting to change the subject and run from reality. 'What happened?' he repeated.

Already the boiling point of his rage was cooling off. Luke regretted his symbolic walkout. 'He put me on the bench,' he said bitterly. Swayne wasn't outraged. Luke stared at him angrily.

'Me? On the bench?' he snarled. 'I'm not being big-headed but I'm ten times better than every single player on that team.' Luke glanced back at his erstwhile team-mates preparing for battle against St Paul's. The sight, sound and smell of football plucked at his heart strings. He was desperate to flip-flop on his decision. He knew a sound reason to return would be provided by his trainer any moment now.

'The problem is . . . you *are* being big-headed. If you really are ten times better than every player on that team, go back, get changed, sit on the bench, then come off it and show them,' Swayne said calmly.

Luke stared at him. It was a super statement. A typical

piece of Swayne mental manipulation. A challenge Luke could not turn his back on. Before he agreed and turned round, his field of vision drifted over Swayne's left shoulder. He stared at the school gates and realised that without the intervention of his trainer they would be fading into the background behind him. Jerome no longer had the power to make him see sense. That responsibility and talent belonged to Peter Swayne. For a moment he wanted to tell him how grateful he—

'Get back over there, Farrell!' Swayne said angrily. 'I haven't worked me arse off for you to blow it now.'

Luke was spared the mushy sentiment. He turned and marched back across the school grounds, marshalled closely by his trainer. It was time to prove certain people wrong and certain people right.

Sitting on the substitutes bench was an interesting experience. Jerome accepted Luke's return without too much drama – although the majority of the players had shifted their allegiance to the Nally faction after his melodramatic display. Even Daniel Popsecu delivered a cold shoulder on the bench. Luke realised he was the outcast, but this hardly bothered him at all. The only thing that concerned him was the presence of the four scouts. They stood as a group near a corner flag, paying considerable attention to Ille.

'Come on, Enders, lift it,' Jerome shouted. The second half was ten minutes old and still scoreless. Luke glanced across at Swayne, who stood away from the main throng of spectators. He knew all about storming off as ex-captain of the Enders. In fact, his presence at home games was something of an affront to the players and staff, who suffered the League Cup Final defeat at the hands of Dalkey United two seasons back.

'No,' Jerome screamed.

Luke turned back to the action on the field. The ball sat in the back of Alan Giles's net. One–nil to St Paul's. Jerome glanced at his temperamental superstar momentarily before concentrating on the pitch and clapping his hands together.

'Come on, lads. Lift it,' he said, pleading passionately.

Luke listened carefully to the words. He realised it was spirits that needed lifting. Team spirit was drowning in the doldrums and he was the main cause of the slump. His self-important behaviour, temper tantrums and mid-season walkabout had ruined the Enders' chances. He thought back to the sparkling unbeaten run at the start of August. Back then he was the captain and inspiration for his team-mates. He would lead by example and encourage them to play for each other.

Now all he cared about was himself. The only reason he wanted to play was to impress the scouts. What happened to the Stretford Enders was irrelevant.

A small group of spectators screamed, 'Yessss!!!' Luke snapped out of his trance. The small group screaming were the subs and staff of St Paul's on the far side of the pitch. They had scored again. Two–nil. Jerome kicked the water bottle in frustration. He turned to Luke, who stared back with a solemn expression. For the first time in months he displayed regret.

'Sorry, boss,' Luke said without thinking.

The undeniable tone of sincerity in his voice struck a chord in Jerome's heart. His original plan was fifteen minutes to reduce the chance of incurring a comeback injury or exposing any lack of match fitness. But something inside said, 'Now.'

'Get warmed up,' he said coldly.

Luke sprang from the bench like a kangaroo. He jinked

past his manager and jogged down the sideline. Several sets of eyes followed him closely. The scouts watched with barely disguised interest. The Enders stared coldly; some spat on the muddy grass as a sign of disgust. Luke came across Swayne, who stood at the corner flag. He looked him straight in the eye. Swayne nodded his head supportively.

'Luke,' Jerome said loudly. He jogged back to his manager's side at the halfway line. Jerome slung a friendly arm round his shoulder. 'I'm putting you on for Ille. Get into centre midfield, make something happen,' he said.

Luke nodded. He took off his tracksuit top and handed it to his manager.

'Ref,' Jerome yelled, waving his left arm about frantically. The referee instructed the St Paul's keeper to pause before taking a goal kick.

'Ille,' Jerome said loudly. This substitution caused a frenzy of mutters and whispers both on and off the pitch. The little Romanian wizard had been the most effective Ender in the match. Now he was making way so golden boy could return.

'Good game, kid,' Jerome said, clutching Ille's head to his chest.

After a six-month absence, Luke Farrell ran back onto the field of play. His legs felt like jelly. He jogged past Lofty and Tosh Pollock to take up position in centre-midfield. This was a test, a test of character.

It was four minutes before Luke got a touch of the ball. The St Paul's players were fine athletes and tremendous competitors. But the one ace up his sleeve was their relative ignorance of his abilities.

'Copper,' he yelled.

Luke knew few of his team-mates would pass the ball to him freely. But Copper Martin was a true captain. Victory for the team meant more to him than individual grudges. Luke was in space on the left wing. Copper knocked a short pass into his path along the floor. The first touch was still intact. Luke controlled the ball effortlessly before poking it through the legs of his marker. That vital burst of speed was also unharmed. He powered past his man, who tried to shoulder-charge him off the ball. He now had a chance to survey the situation. Forty yards from goal with only Con Elliot alone up front. The attack needed further development. Luke dribbled in-field. He weaved his way past a robust challenge from the number seven and a tug of the shirt by the number six before the number four cut off his direct route to goal. This afforded Luke the chance to pick a pass.

'Lofty,' he cried.

Luke chipped a sublime diagonal pass forty yards cross field onto the right boot of Lofty O'Keefe. The rangy right winger was on the edge of the penalty area, one-on-one with the number three.

'Lofty,' Tosh Pollock screamed. The busy central midfielder read the pattern of play perfectly and made a late dart into the penalty area. Lofty heeded the call and laid a simple pass into his path. Tosh decided to hit the ball first time and although he scuffed his shot, he did manage to squeeze it beneath the keeper's body. Two—one.

'Yes. Good stuff,' Jerome yelled.

Luke smiled. It was another perfect phrase from the manager. The presence of the scouts and the pressure to impress suddenly disappeared. All that mattered now was the warm feeling of well-being brewing inside his gut, fermented by football. A saying came to mind, but it wasn't one of Mrs Hendy's. 'You don't know what you've got till it's gone.'

* * *

After Tosh Pollock's goal the match developed into an absolute classic. St Paul's responded bravely and almost snatched a third straight from the kick-off, but before too long the outrageously fresh legs of Luke Farrell got on the ball and began dictating the pattern of play. He set up shop in centre-midfield and sprayed passes left and right. Con Elliot hit the crossbar with a powerful header and Tosh Pollock forced a last-gasp clearance off the line by the number two. An equaliser seemed inevitable.

'Luke,' Nally shouted. His hard-boiled disgust with the former captain cracked after Tosh scored the first goal. Copper Martin's philosophy of team first infected the other Enders. As a result, Luke saw a lot of the ball. Nally's latest pass was a simple ten yarder to feet. Luke was still inside his own half with his back to goal, but it didn't stop his newly detailed man-marker trying to clatter him from behind.

The ref blew for a free-kick.

'Ref,' Nally screamed in protest. He eyeballed the offending midfielder before offering Luke a hand up.

'Cheers,' Luke said. He saw most of the outfield players move into the other half of the field. They were expecting a long punt towards the penalty area. But Luke had other ideas.

'Lay it short,' he whispered to Nally.

When the ref blew his whistle to restart the game, Nally obliged and tipped the ball off to Luke. He bombed forward, shrugging off two weak challenges from the St Paul's front two. Jerome watched in breathless awe as he reproduced the old magic – the kind of skill sadly lacking in the Enders' attacking arsenal over the last six months. Luke dribbled past opposing players with consummate ease. From a position deep in his own half he quickly made a jinking charge to the edge of the opposing penalty area. Seven separate players tried to dispossess him, all to no avail.

'Con,' Luke said loudly. His solo run came to a halt outside the penalty area on the right wing. Performing a dazzling Cruyff flick to wrong-foot two opposing players, Luke checked back and swung a perfectly weighted centre to the far post with his weaker left foot. His intended target was six-foot forward Con Elliot. But instead it was Robert Nally, supporting the attack, who rose highest to head the Enders level.

'Yes, yesss, yesssssss!' Nally screamed in delight. In one majestic moment everything was forgotten. Nally scrambled across to lift Luke into the air. He threw his arms around his former captain's midriff and squeezed him for dear life. The other Enders, substitutes and all, joined in the celebrations. It was Luke who spoiled the party.

'Come on. We can win this,' he said passionately.

Eight minutes remained as a shell-shocked St Paul's kicked off in the centre-circle. All over the pitch the Enders hunted like a pack of rampaging wolves, winning the ball back with pure, savage desire. As soon as they regained possession, the first pass they looked to pick out was to number fourteen, Luke Farrell. Two man-markers shadowed his every move. But this shackle simply inspired him to express the wide range of his creativity.

Luke played everything one-touch. As soon as the ball arrived at his feet he would smash it to a team-mate. Some of these passes were five yards, some were fifty yards, but nearly every one was accurate, reaching its intended target. This constant shift of possession created the space he needed to finish the job. Leslie Ward chased another wonderfully weighted diagonal pass down the left wing into the corner. Luke powered forward to support the attack. Leslie turned back towards his own goal and laid a short pass to Copper, who in turn found Tosh Pollock in space outside the penalty area.

'Tosh,' Luke shouted loudly. The call was unnecessary. Tosh had spotted his charge into the penalty area and the ball was already in flight when he called. Luke concentrated on the incoming cross, ignoring everything else. He swooped low, diving like a bird of prey, and redirecting the flight of the ball with the merest glance of his forehead.

'Oh no,' Swayne said fearfully.

The ball was in the back of the net. Some of the Enders were celebrating their three–two lead, but most of them rushed to the scene of the scrum. Luke was lodged between three bodies. The goalkeeper, the number four and the number six were piled on top of his back. Jerome and Swayne charged onto the pitch together.

'Luke, Luke,' Jerome cried.

Twenty-plus people were standing in the St Paul's penalty area, all of them silent. The irony was horrendous. Nally and Tosh felt a deep swelling of guilt in their guts. The player they regarded as a selfish egomaniac looking out for number one had just won the game with a remarkable act of bravery which resulted in him being crushed in a keeper/centre-half sandwich. Luke had been so determined to score for the Enders that he ignored the inevitable collision with the onrushing goalkeeper and covering defenders. It was the kind of bravery Mark Hughes and Alan Shearer were renowned for – going in where it hurts, to hell with the consequences. It was a quality that all truly great goal scorers possessed. The desire to score became so strong, it tended to override all other concerns; even personal injury took a back seat. The St Paul's goalkeeper was unconscious. The number four clutched his right arm in agony and the number six staggered to his feet in a daze.

'Luke,' Jerome said softly.

For a moment, everyone thought he was dead. But after lying motionless on the ground for a whole minute, Luke sat up slowly, stretched his back, then jumped to his feet. His team-mates and manager stared at him as if he had just risen from the dead. It took a bright smile and a fist raised in celebration to snap them from their daze.

'What are you all staring at?' Luke said sharply. 'This game's not over yet.'

While St Paul's tended to their wounded trio, Luke jogged back to the centre-circle. The other Enders eventually followed suit. By now, Peter Swayne wore a smile as wide as O'Connell Street bridge. Jerome didn't share his expression. His face was pallid. Before leaving the field he blessed himself and whispered a little prayer to God.

'Thanks, boss,' he said quietly.

The home dressing room was a hive of activity after the match. A mate of Nally's called on his mobile to report the unexpected news that Valley Rangers had suffered a shock one–nil home defeat to lowly Ashwood Celtic. This meant the Stretford Enders topped Division B on goal difference with two league games left to play. Luke sat in the middle of it all, soaking up every second as if it were his last. Jerome was still outside with the scouts. He approached them as a group for a chat after the game.

'Luke,' Nally said.

Luke focused on Nally and Tosh Pollock standing in front of him. It was a committee-led apology.

'Welcome back,' they said in unison, offering their hands for shaking.

Luke obliged. 'Thanks,' he said, smiling at his reclaimed team-mates with a new sense of respect. He had deserved the treatment they dished out pre-match. Some might say their sudden turnaround was a weak gesture based purely on his performance. But it wasn't about good and bad players. It was about players who played for the team.

Jerome appeared at the dressing-room door. He gave Luke a subtle nod. 'Right, lads, great effort today. I'll see you Tuesday night,' he said happily.

Luke took his kit bag and walked out the dressing-room door alone. He followed Jerome down the corridor to a secluded alcove behind a row of metal lockers. He looked at his manager anxiously. 'What did they say?'

Jerome grimaced at the question. Luke couldn't believe it. After all he had been through in the last six months, the effort and commitment invested to win back all he had thrown away – after all that, bad news caught up with him at the finish line to ruin everything.

'Well, I don't want you to get downhearted,' Jerome said awkwardly.

Luke looked at him intently. What Jerome couldn't face telling him was the four scouts had walked off with the words 'Thanks, but no thanks.'

Luke decided to accept the reality. A career in professional football had finally slipped away from him for good. Perhaps it slipped away last August in Liverpool, or last October in the final minutes of the Underwood Athletic match. But it had definitely slipped away.

'It's OK, boss. I understand,' he said.

'No, it's not like that, kid,' Jerome replied optimistically. 'There's always next season, or an Irish League club—'

Luke cut across his manager. 'It's OK,' he said sharply. It wasn't anger or bitterness in his voice. He stared at Jerome with a bright smile.

'Next season there's Division A of the South Dublin

League,' Luke said proudly.

Jerome smiled. In the privacy of the alcove they embraced. After six months apart, Luke was more than satisfied to win back his club, his team-mates and his manager. Anything else would be downright greedy.

'I've got to run,' he said.

Jerome nodded his head. 'See you Tuesday, kid.'

Luke took one last look before turning and walking down the corridor. Inside, his heart was broken, but he was determined to recover and play on with his team-mates in Division A of the South Dublin League. At that moment in time, he couldn't help but ponder the bad luck which had twice stolen his shot at the dream. As soon as he had departed Jerome plucked his Nokia mobile from his jacket pocket and made a call. It was just another busy day in the life of a football manager/sports store owner.

Outside the dressing rooms, Swayne waited patiently for Luke's arrival. He wore a confident smile, which drooped as soon as he saw the disappointment in Luke's eyes. Before he could ask the question he received an answer.

'I'll tell you on the bus,' Luke said quietly.

They walked from the school grounds side by side as the day of destiny swung its focus from him to Swayne. It was time to set the Cecilia trap.

LOOK AT ME NOW

Luke stood outside the door of the male changing rooms backstage at the RDS, reading the *Daily Star*. To his surprise and tempered delight he noticed the name of Tonka Matthews in the Ireland U-18 squad to face Spain in a European Championship qualifier at Tolka Park. It brought a smile then a frown in the same motion. Like so many things in life, bitter and sweet were walking hand in hand.

'Nice one, Tonk,' Luke muttered quietly.

All around him people ran, screamed and shouted as if someone had been assassinated. It was a startling sight. Fabulous female models in various states of undress flanked by make-up artists, wardrobe managers and general hangers-on. In such a hectic atmosphere it was only a matter of time before the blonde witch reared her ugly head. Swayne appeared from the changing room with his hair spiked towards the ceiling. He looked like someone with four thousand volts running through their veins, decked out in black PVC trousers and something that resembled a chain-mail vest.

'Any sign?' he said quietly.

Luke shook his head, still rendered speechless by the startling sight before him. Swayne glanced left while chewing on his right thumbnail.

Luke slapped his hand in a consciously gruff male fashion. 'Cut that out,' he said sternly. 'Do you know how much manicures cost?' He wore a smug smile. Swayne wasn't amused. He puffed out a nervous sigh. Luke felt the need to talk some last-minute tactics. He tugged Swayne's arm.

'Hey. Remember what I said. When you see her, you're too busy to talk.'

Swayne nodded. He was miles away mentally, pre-occupied with the show or Cecilia. In the meantime, Luke observed the amorous glares fired the way of his trainer by the barrage of female models who passed by. It was another creepy repeat of the scene in the Vortex. David Swayne and his brother had more in common than they could ever imagine, that much was clear from Luke's perspective: the overwhelming sense of insecurity. Both brothers found remarkably different ways to mask this vulnerability: foot-balling brilliance and outright thuggery. But in the end, it was something at the core of their personalities, something they could never escape. The weight of this ailment on his shoulders had forced David over the edge. Luke would have to stop its march on Peter.

'Peter,' he said quietly.

Swayne spun to face Luke and watched him intently for some words of wisdom. In Luke's throat was a short speech about the illness of moping after Cecilia. There were bright and exciting horizons to be chased away from her wicked influence. If he continued to invest his energy in such an empty venture it would hollow out all the virtues of Peter Swayne hidden from the world. Luke was on the verge of beginning the speech, but could go no further.

'Good luck today,' he said weakly.

Swayne smiled. He joined the other male models, who piled out of the dressing room in single file and walked to the starting point at the side of the stage. A round of applause swelled in stature from the audience out front and the music started to pound the walls and ceiling. Luke had been on the verge when some words came back to haunt him: 'If you're determined to destroy all our hard work, there's nothing I can do to stop you.' The words that had saved him from oblivion could well condemn the man who spoke them. If Peter Swayne were to save himself from the pit of despair, he would do it alone. Luke knew the solution, but until Swayne figured it out for himself, he would remain in the dark.

Luke had one last duty to perform to help snare the blonde witch in his tangled web. While the male models did their thing on the catwalk, he took up a position on the left-hand side of the backstage area. With their male counterparts halfway through the show, the female models began appearing from their dressing room, taking position in the wings for finishing touches to their make-up and first costumes. It was only a matter of time before a set of eyes spotted him.

'What are you doing here?' Cecilia said in surprise.

Luke casually spun his head round to greet her. She walked across to investigate his presence, wearing a stunning chequered PVC boob-tube, mini-skirt combo. Her hair was tied in kinky pigtails.

'All right,' Luke replied with a pleasant smile.

Cecilia placed both hands on her shapely hips. She wanted an explanation. She was about to get it. 'How did *you* get backsta—?'

Before she could finish her question, a sight to behold headed towards her from the catwalk, receiving rapturous applause every confident step of the way. Luke folded his arms, stood back a couple of feet and allowed nature to take its course.

'P-P-Peter,' Cecilia stuttered in astonishment.

Swayne held his nerve brilliantly. Upon his exit from the stage he smiled happily and pulled an expensive designer jumper over his head. 'Fancy seeing you here,' he said with a wonderful sense of disregard.

Cecilia was sunk. She had no plausible comeback. Swayne didn't glance at Luke for guidance. He didn't need any on-the-spot coaching. The master had prepared his pupil well and his presence was no longer necessary.

'Well, I'd better be off. See you round, kids,' Luke said before walking away from the scene of victory. After making his way across the backstage area to the fire exit, he stopped to check on the progress of the trap. He chuckled to himself as Cecilia scuttled after Swayne, desperate for his attention. He played an absolute blinder, fending off her approach with a determined walk to the door of the male dressing room and a polite smile and verbal explanation followed by a blunt exit. Cecilia stood outside the dressing room, spurned by a firm sweep of the door in her face.

'Game, set, match, championship,' Luke said happily. He pushed down on the safety bar and shoved the fire exit door open. The deal struck between himself and Swayne at the end of January was complete. There was nothing left to say or do. With this in mind, Luke needed to pay some people a visit.

Living with Yourself

Luke sat on the 46A that afternoon in a state of satisfaction. Despite the disappointment of the morning he still felt a sense of achievement and renewal. Whatever sadness he had suffered in failing to impress a set of scouts was offset by the journey he had made from his perch in the pit of despair in early January. He had regained football, a positive outlook on life and the ability to laugh and smile. These advances were far more important than a career in professional football. Luke came to that conclusion sincerely.

It was ten past five when he hopped off the 46A at the top of the Stillorgan dual carriageway. It was a bright spring evening and he fancied a leisurely stroll to pass the time. Back in the RDS, both Swayne and D'Argo would be networking or tying up deals. It brought a hint of sadness to mind at the thought of Swayne and Cecilia. Luke would have to accept his part in Swayne's eventual downfall. His period in the sun would be all too brief. Before long, Cecilia would move on to pastures new, as always. It was inevitable.

Deansgrange cemetery was dotted with visitors laying flowers and wreaths at headstones. The usual description of graveyards as morbid always struck Luke as a misnomer. He always felt at peace there. A soothing serenity surrounded the marble headstones. He could hear the soft background noise of traffic on the road outside and the sweet song of a lark close by. The black marble headstone that marked Mrs

Hendy's final resting place sparkled in the early evening sunlight. Luke crouched down to lay a bunch of white carnations he had bought from Daley's newsagent's in Foxrock. He exhaled happily and smiled at the thought of his special friend. A visit to the back parlour, tea and cake and the countless words of advice.

'I really miss you, Mrs H,' Luke said quietly. He wasn't aware of anyone nearby. But if someone were to overhear his comment to the damp earth below it wouldn't have bothered him in the slightest.

'I didn't make it, Mrs H. Remember how I promised to make it?' Luke said. He glanced up at the blue sky above. 'Well, I gave it my best shot. It just . . . wasn't to be,' he concluded sadly.

Luke smiled. If she were still alive and he had to break the news of his failure, she would respond immediately with the advice, 'Chin up, shoulders straight.' Pride and dignity were the most important qualities to retain, even in your darkest hour. No, *especially* in your darkest hour. It was what the British called 'a stiff upper lip'. A virtuous state of mind. Even though she had passed on to the next world, Mrs Hendy's influence and philosophy lived on inside his mind and soul. In the short space of time they had been friends she had instilled in him a special kind of drive and determination. The heavy burden of a broken leg, David's death and Ella's departure had eroded that state of mind. But as if sent by special delivery from the heavens, Peter Swayne had revived those beliefs.

Luke moved across the cemetery to the sight of David Swayne's final resting place. Daylight seemed to dip as he made the short journey north along a gravel path. He glanced at the white marble headstone, breathing deeply to keep his composure. Speaking to Mrs Hendy in the skies above wasn't upsetting, but contacting David with words floating into thin air sent a shiver up his spine.

'You shouldn't be here,' he said sadly. No one argued to the contrary.

'If I weren't such a selfish bastard . . . you'd be alive.' Luke suddenly realised the irony. 'And me and Peter would still be enemies.' The death of David Swayne had sent the lives of himself and Peter off on drastic detours. It was a horrible thought to contemplate. Out of the tragedy they had rescued something undeniably worthwhile: a friendship that gave both parties a second chance at living.

Luke shuffled uncomfortably. 'I wish you were alive,' he said vacantly.

Silence commanded the conversation for a long period of time. Luke's plan to clear his conscience once and for all had backfired badly. The guilt he had intended to eradicate with a heartfelt confession found a new seed to nurture and cultivate in the dark plains of his mind. Out of David's death he still found a way to prosper. The shame was too much to bear. He began to walk away from the headstone. Inside, the bile of self-loathing was consuming tissue at an alarming rate. The only remedy seemed to be a large injection of sugar- and salt-based snack treats, followed by the swift delivery of some takeaway bounty. Luke was outside the side entrance to the cemetery when he found the courage to grind to a halt. He spun round and glanced back tentatively at the headstones behind the perimeter wall. This was no time to run away, this was a time to stand and fight. With a fresh sense of determination, he marched back to the headstone.

'Yeah, I've come out on top as usual,' he said angrily. 'But that doesn't mean I'm happy.'

Luke paced from side to side, breathing rapidly. 'I should

have helped you. I know that,' he pleaded. He stared at the headstone, tears began to roll down his cheek. 'I'm sorry, David. I'm sorry.'

He leaned his right hand against the top of the headstone. It was all he could say. There was no way to make up for David's death. He was gone. All that Luke could do was apologise and move on with his life. The way Tonka, Jerome and even Peter Swayne had done. He lifted himself up and wiped the tears from his eyes. He placed a single red rose by the foot of the headstone and bowed his head respectfully. Quietly, he sang 'You'll Never Walk Alone' as day turned to night in Deansgrange cemetery.

Luke reached D'Argo's palace shortly after eight that evening. Night had fallen. The security gates slowly retracted to allow him onto the driveway. A single light lit the porch outside and a single light illuminated the kitchen. He expected to find the house empty, with D'Argo and Martina still wining and dining at the RDS. The plan for the evening was simple: *Taxi Driver* started on BBC 2 at ten past ten. Beforehand Luke would catch up on his e-mail with Ronald and pay a passing visit to the *FHM* website to view some pictures. When he opened the front door, the *beep-beep* of the armed alarm system never materialised. Instead, a group of voices rushed at him from the kitchen.

'Luke,' Martina said loudly. Surprise number one. Luke closed the front door behind him.

'Yeah,' he replied casually. He walked from the hallway into the kitchen before stopping in shock.

Jerome sat at the kitchen counter, nursing a smug smile and a steaming cup of coffee. Sitting beside him was a small, stout man with a bald head. He was wearing a navy promo jacket and a pleasant smile.

'Luke. This is Terry Wise, director of Tottenham's youth academy,' Jerome said happily.

Terry rose from his stool and shook Luke's hand. 'A pleasure, son,' he said in a strong Cockney accent.

Luke was speechless. He caught sight of a set of stapled sheets in Terry's left hand. Martina stood by the fridge wearing a proud smile, fighting back a tear or two. Jerome clicked his silver Parker ballpoint on and off playfully.

'I've been talking it over with Jerome and your mum,' Terry said with a serious expression. 'We'd like to offer you a two-year stay at the youth academy.'

Luke could hardly find the strength to smile. His legs seemed to buckle beneath him. Terry offered a helping hand as he leaned to the counter to steady himself. It wasn't the greatest reaction to such breathtaking news. But until the reality sank in, a dreamlike state would have to suffice.

'Erm, where – where do I sign?' Luke said in between gasps for air.

Jerome handed him his Parker and directed his attention to the dotted line on page four of the contract. Terry placed a friendly hand on Luke's shoulder and smiled as he scribbled his signature beneath his mother's and Jerome's.

'That's the first of many autographs you'll sign, son,' he said confidently. Jerome laughed. Terry and Martina smiled.

Luke turned to all three and raised his hand. 'I'm sorry about this,' he said politely.

'YESSSSSSSSSSSSSSSSSSSSS!!!!!!!!!!!'

Terry Wise stayed for two hours after Luke's delighted outburst. He complimented the brave manner in which he had risked injury to win the game for the Enders. He gave mother and son a rundown on the youth academy's state-of-the-art facilities in Islington. Accommodation, treatment room, education courses – Tottenham Hotspur was a club firmly fixed in the twenty-first century when it came to youth team development. After a firm handshake, Terry bid Martina, Jerome and Luke farewell. He arranged to collect his new signing from Heathrow Airport in six weeks' time. Every minute in between would be tortuously long.

When the dust settled, Luke and Jerome faced one another on the doorstep. The sneaky exploits of his manager had come to the fore over the course of Terry's two-hour visit. He spilled the beans on Jerome's six-month period of harassment – phone calls, faxes, e-mails, demanding the return of Terry and the other three scouts in April to review the talents of Luke Farrell.

'Thanks, boss,' Luke said happily. 'Thanks for everything.'

Jerome smiled. 'Not your boss for much longer,' he replied. The pride was palpable. They embraced each other like father and son. It had been a long, dark tunnel. But now, finally, they were crawling to the end, and the light was shining through brightly. And yet again, in the same breath, there was a footnote of sadness to the celebration. Luke had played his last game as a Stretford Ender.

'I'll see you Tuesday,' Jerome said before walking along the driveway. Luke watched him go. It was the end of a beautiful era – one he would never forget as long as he lived. But with each ending comes a new beginning.

'Glory, glory, Tottenham Hotspur,' Jerome chanted before he disappeared through the security gates.

After fifteen minutes of tears, hugs, kisses and a few more tears thrown in to boot, Luke escaped the loving clutch of Martina and retired to his bedroom balcony to celebrate. He revved up Jay's old record player and grooved, time and time again, to the supercool instrumental 'Wade in the Water' by Ramsey Lewis and his slick orchestra. At the same time, he powered up the Fujitsu PC and sent off an e-mail to Ronald, relaying the wonderful news. It was half eleven when he thought of ringing Peter Swayne's mobile. After a second to contemplate the likely interruption of a sensual clinch with Cecilia, he decided to wait until the morning to break the news. He grooved around his room a little longer, cranking up the speakers to full pelt and opening the patio door to allow a breath of sea breeze to join the party.

'Woo,' Luke yelled in agreement with Ramsey. He could barely make out the heavy thump-thump on his bedroom door or the scream of 'Luke!' It was only when the door opened and Martina stood aside to let Swayne in that he came to his senses. When he saw Swayne, it was clear by the smile on his face that Martina had already imparted the news of Tottenham Hotspur.

'Spurs, baby, yeah,' Luke screamed. He grooved from the balcony to his bedroom and invited his mother to boogie. For the first time in years Luke actually managed to embarrass Martina with his actions rather than the other way round. She slapped his wrist playfully and made a half-dignified exit. Swayne sat down on the corner of Luke's bed and waited for Ramsey Lewis to finish doing his thing before speaking. At the end of the song, he explained his late appearance at D'Argo's palace.

'Sorry for calling so late,' he said pointlessly. Luke's adrenaline-filled delirium faded without its groovy sound-track. He sat against his computer desk and faced Swayne. Something was wrong.

'What's going on?' he asked bluntly.

Swayne scratched his forehead. 'There's an after-show party in the Pod. Free drink, food, the works,' he explained.

'Do you fancy coming along?'

Now this was a shock to the system. Luke had to ask the obvious question.

'Does Cecilia know about this?' he said.

'Why?' Swayne replied.

'Well, won't I be something of a third wheel?'

Swayne bowed his head to hide a sneaky little smile. Luke sensed a fresh development. He chased after the truth like a morally-minded news reporter.

'What happened?' he said.

Swayne looked up. 'Shit, shower, shave. I'll explain on the way to the Pod.'

Twenty minutes later, just a scratch off midnight, Luke and Swayne prepared to leave his bedroom. A night of celebration in an exclusive nightclub surrounded by a truck-load of beautiful young waif-like models meant little to Luke. He had one desire – to unlock the dark secret hidden inside Swayne's mind.

'Come on, tell me what happened,' he demanded as they walked along the hall. Swayne stopped so sharply Luke bumped into his back. He turned and placed his index finger against his lip to ensure silence. Luke was speechless, anyway. On the invitation of his trainer, he tiptoed forward to view a sight. Standing at the kitchen counter were Martina and Jude, chatting over a cup of tea. It was a startling sight, but one Luke didn't completely understand. He and Swayne shuffled back down the hall to his bedroom door.

'What about you and Cecilia?' Luke said in a whisper.

Swayne stared at him happily. 'There is no me and Cecilia. Not since I met Jude.'

Now Luke was completely confused. The whole scenario

had a scent of Baring's Bank and Nick Leeson to it. The sums just didn't add up.

'But you ran off on her,' Luke said clumsily.

Swayne nodded. 'I know. But not because of Jude,' he replied. Luke shook his head in muddled agreement. Swayne offered further explanation.

'I ran off because I wanted to see this thing through. Now it's over, I can be with Jude.'

Luke was getting with the programme. Swayne wanted to hit Cecilia with the sting. The whole point of the RDS Spring Show was winning the battle of wills, claiming the right to have the final say on their doomed love affair.

'So, you told Cecilia to get stuffed?' Luke ventured cautiously.

Swayne wore a devilish smile. 'Right in front of Giovanni. She grabbed my arm, refused to let me leave.'

Luke burst out laughing. At last, justice had been served on the blonde witch. The super minx had been put in her place by the last person in the world she could ever have expected to turn down her advances.

' "How dare you walk away from me! You love me, Peter Swayne. We were meant to be together," ' he mimed comically.

Luke folded up in creases. It was a good thirty seconds before he calmed down. When he found some semblance of control, Swayne changed the tone of their discussion.

'Thanks,' he said solemnly.

'For what?' Luke replied.

Swayne was overcome with happiness. He put his hand on Luke's left shoulder. 'For everything,' he said.

In the concealing twilight of the hall the two boys embraced each other as true friends. Together they had climbed from the pit of despair and together they could now stare up at the sun and smile. Finally, they walked from the hall into the kitchen.

Jude and Martina turned to them with smiles.

'Congratulations,' Jude said to Luke. He nodded his head and watched Swayne walk to her side and place his arm around her waist.

'Same to you,' Luke replied wryly.

Martina had to bite her tongue not to comment. Luke spared her blushes and clapped his hands together.

'We'd better make a move,' he said happily.

Swayne and Jude walked to the front door entwined as one. Luke glanced at his mother and winked. She ushered the three teenagers through the front door and wished them a pleasant night – what was left of it. Luke, Swayne and Jude walked from the driveway and headed downhill towards the Killiney Court Hotel and the main office of South City Cabs, laughing and joking all the way. They all had excellent reasons to be happy. Especially the newest trainee at Tottenham Hotspur. He had become aware of the need to live life in the moment. As things stood, then and there, he was happy. In the future he would face certain sadness and disappointment. But melancholy would have to wait its turn for a run in the first team. Until that day came, the sun could continue to shine.

THE
STRETFORD
ENDERS
BY
TREVOR J. COLGAN

Luke Farrell is fed up with his mother,
Martina. Just as his football team has
made it to the semi-finals of the All
Ireland Schoolboys' League, Martina
has decided to uproot them both and move
to Dun Laoghaire. For her it means a new job – perhaps
a new man. But for Luke it means the end of his
footballing dream and a struggle to fit in at Woodlawn
School.

Can Cecilia of the candy-floss hair be trusted? Might Swayne,
her bullying boyfriend, beat him to a pulp? Is the enigmatic
Ella really a Man City fan or just posing? And will Luke be
able to create a half-decent football team from the dross of
Dun Laoghaire?

RED FOX
ISBN 0 09 940927 5

THE STRETFORD ENDERS AWAY

BY TREVOR J. COLGAN

'Playing away can push even the best players beyond the limit.'

Luke Farrell is leaving for Liverpool. He stands at the stern of the Stena Seacat and watches Dublin fade into the mist.

Luke has got his heart's desire – a trial with Everton. But his struggle for stardom has strained his friendships at home. And as he moves towards the bright lights and glory of Goodison Park, his girlfriend, Ella, fades into the shadows.

A future of football and fame is Luke's goal. But Fate has other plans for him. So has a girl called Stacey Culshaw. And by the end of the scorching summer his heart will be torn in two across the Irish Sea.

A tremendous follow-up to Trevor J. Colgan's powerful debut novel, *The Stretford Enders*.

RED FOX
ISBN 0 09 941704 9